Chapter One

Dylan was sweating.

It was the kind of hot and sticky sweat that just doesn't feel good. Especially not when your aircon is broken. Dylan didn't have the money to get it fixed either.

It was problem after problem.

What made it worse was that he was due on air for a cam show any minute. The clock was against him as he tried to wipe the sweat from his brow and take on some much-needed water.

Urgh. I wish I didn't have to do this.

This is definitely not why I moved to New York.

Dylan let out a long sigh.

He was twenty-two and had dreams of acting on Broadway. Hustling for tips on online cam shows for dirty old men was about as far away from that dream as he could imagine.

It wasn't a good situation.

Dylan didn't judge anyone who did cam shows. Each and every person probably had their own unique reason for doing it.

1

Dylan was no different either.

But it was getting to a point where he was really hating it.

The apartment was looking a little grimy.

Well, that was an understatement.

Ever since he moved in, the apartment just didn't look especially clean or fresh. It wasn't through want of trying. Dylan had attempted several deep cleans. But no matter what he tried, he just couldn't get the place looking as fresh as he would have wanted.

It was a small, not especially comfortable corner apartment on the seventh floor of the building. It still had high ceilings, which was one positive thing. But other than that, it really wasn't much to write home about.

Dylan had attempted to make it a little more homely by putting up his paintings and favorite coloring book drawings. His one sanctuary was his bedroom which he had painted light blue and pink and decorated with some cute fairy lights.

It was something at least.

But still, Dylan was never able to shake the feeling that the apartment was more a place he lived and not a *home*.

Dylan had tried to speak to his landlord but hadn't got anywhere. The problem was that he could only just about afford to pay for this place. The kind of buildings that had airier, cleaner apartments were simply out of his financial reach.

Speaking of finances...

Dylan's problem had always been managing money.

He just wasn't very good at matching his expenditure to his income. Well, that's an understatement. Dylan was actually *terrible* with money.

Like, *seriously* bad.

2

Even in high school Dylan had managed to run up debts. To this day, he was still paying off credit cards from years ago. Clothes, coffee, trips and enjoying the nightlife all cost money. Dylan didn't have the discipline to hold back on any of them.

Dylan had always figured that when he was a big Broadway actor, money would be no issue. He wouldn't even need to manage his expenses and outgoings, someone would do that for him. Like an agent or accountant.

Dylan's cell phone flashed.

It was a message from his friend Casper.

Hey! We're coloring and playing our favorite games? Want to come? Caspy XoXo

Dylan sighed. He would have loved to join Casper for some coloring and painting fun.

But he couldn't.

The rent was very much overdue at this point and Dylan had already received two warnings from the building manager.

Hanging out with Casper was something that had really kept Dylan going through the recent tough times. As a fellow Little, Casper understood exactly what to say and do to keep spirits up.

Provide the sunshine in the dark times.

Always know when it was time for a sleepover and movie night.

Dylan was lucky to have such a great friend. He only wished Casper could do something about getting him a connection with some theatre producers.

Oh well, Casper was a great friend but even he couldn't help with that!

I don't wanna do this.

I really, really don't...

Dylan felt anxious and a little bit sad too.

His relationship with camming was complex. It was how he had met his previous Daddy.

Initially, it had all seemed like fun.

There was a sexual connection and after performing several shows, Dylan had agreed to meet up. But far from being a caring and protective Daddy, the man in question was simply interested in sex.

Just sex.

Nothing else.

It wasn't what Dylan craved. Anyone could have sex. That wasn't what a Daddy and Little relationship was all about for Dylan. He wanted to experience a *deeper* connection.

Discipline...

Love...

Protection...

Fun and snuggles...

What made this so-called Daddy even worse in Dylan's eyes was that he wanted to share Dylan. Pass him around other Daddy Doms. Dylan hadn't liked this. In fact, he *hated* it.

Dylan felt like he was being used and the relationship came to an abrupt end. He couldn't deal with being in a situation where he didn't feel loved or appreciated.

The only problem was that Dylan struggled to move on. He felt scarred by the experience. Worse, Dylan started to feel unable to trust people.

Especially when it came to potential new relationships.

Dylan saw his cell phone flash again. It wasn't a message this time, it was his alarm buzzing to tell him that it was nearly cam time.

'Yuck,' Dylan said, 'Hopefully I can make some decent money today.'

Dylan shot a glance over to Pinky, his favorite stuffie.

'You don't judge me, right?' Dylan said. 'One day I won't have to do this. I hope.'

Pinky, a cuddly little pink teddy, didn't reply. He just stared back as he always did.

One of Dylan's favorite hobbies was taking Pinky and the rest of his collection of stuffies and making them put on shows for him. He would do all of the voices himself and have a really fun time. It was his way of living out his Broadway dreams.

Dreams that had once felt a lot closer to reality...

Dylan thought back to the day he heard he had been cast in Island Life, a big new musical. It had been the greatest day of his life. It was like all of his dreams coming true in one phone call.

All of the years spent working on his singing. His dancing. Not to mention his acting too. Dylan had spent *thousands* of dollars on classes.

Sadly, Island Life had its funding pulled at the last minute and Dylan didn't get to experience the Broadway lights even once.

It had been a terrible, bitter blow to his confidence too.

The theatre company losing its funding wasn't Dylan's fault, he knew that. But part of him felt like it had been fate. Just a sign from the universe that his career wasn't meant to be.

It was after the show crashed and burned that Casper had suggested Dylan try cam work. Just temporarily. The idea being that a new Broadway part would come along pretty soon.

Sadly, it hadn't worked out like that. Not even close. It was like the more desperate Dylan got, the worse his auditions went. He simply couldn't catch a break.

Deep down, Dylan would never give up on his dream. But right at that moment, it felt so distant he may as well have done.

'Okay, here goes,' Dylan said, stripping down and getting into his very skimpy cam costume.

With his big, hazel eyes and dirty blond hair, Dylan had always gotten attention from men. His soft, plump lips combined with his innocent expression made him a bit of a standout.

This was to his advantage in the cam world.

The men that came looking for guys like Dylan wanted someone innocent and slender. Dylan knew this and although he didn't enjoy flirting with gross men, he did it so that he could pay his rent and put food in his mouth.

Sometimes, the tips could be great.

If it meant that he could afford a trip to the movies that was super.

Or even better treat his friends to a super-sized milkshake with all the sprinkles.

All said, Dylan was happy enough to flash his smile and show a little more of his body if it made life outside the apartment more fun.

Dylan looked at himself in the mirror.

His see-through plastic crop-top highlighted his slender, smooth torso. The micro-shorts left little to the imagination too, perfectly showing off his peachy butt.

Just as Dylan was about to log onto the cam server, he heard a noise.

The creaking of his apartment door.

Huh, what the hell?

Dylan turned around and saw that it was his landlord. He immediately blushed and attempted to cover himself up a little by grabbing a pillow from the couch.

'I'm here to fix the aircon,' the landlord said, his eyes wandering all over Dylan, desperate to catch a glimpse. 'Unless you're too busy?'

Dylan felt so uncomfortable.

The landlord was a slimy guy.

Not someone who Dylan wanted to spend a second longer with than he absolutely had to.

But on the other hand, he desperately needed the aircon to work again. It was summer. The heat and humidity weren't going to go anywhere. This was a problem that needed sorting out as soon as possible.

'N-n-n-no, it's fine,' Dylan said, edging back toward the kitchen area as the landlord walked behind him and then over toward the aircon unit. 'T-t-t-thank you for coming. It's been broken for a while.'

Dylan felt nervous.

The landlord reminded Dylan a little bit of his old Daddy. It was clear that he had no interest in Dylan as a person. All he did was see a sexual object who also happened to be his tenant.

'This is an old unit, but this fix should keep it going,' the landlord said, his voice distracted as he worked a screwdriver hard inside the white plastic casing. 'Oh, and while I'm here, I have some news.'

'Oh, okay?' Dylan said, his heart-rate increasing.

'Yeah, rent's going up,' the landlord said, not showing a single shred of emotion or empathy. 'Has to be done. That's just the way things are going all over the city. Us poor landlords are facing increased costs across the board. Like, you know, having to fix appliances in our properties?'

OMG, is he trying to make a joke?

Dylan couldn't quite believe that the landlord was being so flippant. But his irritation at that aside, Dylan immediately began to panic.

How the hell was he going to be able to cope with a rent increase?

After all, the current rent was pushing him to his limits.

He could barely afford it.

A single cent more and Dylan knew he was in real danger of losing the apartment.

The landlord's visit was going from bad to worse.

'I take it you don't have an issue with that?'

'Um, n-n-n-no, that's fine,' Dylan replied.

Dylan wasn't very good at dealing with conflict.

Never had been.

He was trying to figure out in his head if the landlord was even allowed to put the rent up like that.

But Dylan just didn't have the courage to ask him.

'You know, there are other arrangements we could come to?' the landlord said, turning to face Dylan and licking his lips.

Dylan felt sick.

This was *horrible*. Totally gross in fact.

'No, I'll pay, it's fine, I promise,' Dylan stuttered, tripping over his words.

But Dylan was anything but comfortable.

He had no idea how he would cope with paying more rent. Sure, he could put in more time on the cams, but that would take away from his practice time for singing and acting.

He had classes that he went to.

Improvisation workshops.

Plus, Dylan wanted to make sure that he still saw his friends. More time on the cams would eat away into his life.

And he already hated it doing it part time.

More hours would just be awful.

The landlord took one more leering look at Dylan before heading out of the apartment. At least the aircon issue was sorted out. That was one bonus at least.

'Oh, here's your mail,' the landlord said, just before he left. 'Don't say I never do you any favors!'

Dylan rolled his eyes.

What a load of rubbish. He was a horrible landlord.

'Thank you,' Dylan said, taking the small pile of envelopes and shutting the door firmly.

Alone in his apartment and already running a little late for the first cam show, Dylan opened the first envelope.

No. No way. What the...

Dylan couldn't believe what he was looking at.

It was a photo of him. Naked. His body totally exposed as he lay back on his bed. The photo had clearly been taken through his window somehow.

This was disgusting.

It was also totally terrifying.

Dylan may not have enjoyed doing the cam work but at least he always felt safe.

Protected by the privacy of his apartment.

But this put everything into doubt.

Dylan felt his stomach churn and his heart thump and thud inside his ribcage.

He was panicking.

His mind running with possibilities and none of them good.

Knowing that he had to put it to the back of his mind

ahead of his cam session was one thing, but in practice it seemed impossible to ignore the facts.

Someone had been spying on Dylan and had taken the most compromising photos possible.

They almost certainly had more where this one had come from.

They could have been of more sexy and naughty acts too. The kind of things that Dylan would only do for extra money.

Dylan was truly terrified.

Who the hell had been watching him?

And was this just the beginning?

Chapter Two

Flint Maddox was pissed.

Seriously irritated by the pile of police paperwork on his desk, Flint wanted to be out on the streets. Not cooped up in his office.

With a heatwave across the city, the NYC police department buildings were hot, sticky, and full of grumpy cops.

Not exactly a laid-back atmosphere.

Still, the work *had* to be done.

There was no avoiding it.

'Kaplinski, you got that homicide file I asked for?' Flint called out.

'Nah, hasn't come in yet,' Detective Kaplinski called back, busy with his own work.

'Jesus Damned Christ,' Flint grumbled. 'Would it kill anyone to do *anything* on time? Don't answer that!'

Flint was in his mid-thirties.

Being a cop was in his blood.

A family tradition.

One that he had been more than keen to take on and run with for another generation.

But life as a cop was never easy.

There was always a new drama lurking around the corner.

A new case.

A new series of problems that needed solving.

Flint could be grouchy and cynical at the best of times, but on a hot day it seemed like he was close to boiling over at any moment.

Flint leaned back in his chair and drained the remaining iced coffee from the plastic container.

Details of his latest case spun around in his head.

He needed to think.

Flint needed to put his thoughts together.

Nothing had been the same for Flint since he lost a younger police partner a few years earlier. Mickie Roldo was his name. They had been a good team. The chemistry just right. The kind of chemistry that had begun to spill over into their personal lives.

It had been a vice bust that had gone wrong. *Badly* wrong. When his partner died, Flint felt like a part of him went too.

Sure, he still wanted to be a cop.

It was all he knew.

But something about his partner's death had brought out his cynical, pessimistic side. Ever since that fateful day, life had felt like a struggle.

As such, Flint rarely smiled.

This was a shame, because Flint was undeniably a very handsome man. He was tall, and naturally equipped with the kind of physique that most men would kill for.

He was truly ripped.

Chiseled from head to toe.

He didn't even work out all that much anymore. By this point his body had just become one solid piece of finely tuned muscle mass.

Flint was about as far from the stereotype of the fat, donut-munching cop as you could get.

But this wasn't the only difference.

Flint also wouldn't have been seen dead in the crumpled, stale old suits that most beat detectives wore either.

No, Flint was a man of style.

He prided himself on showing up each and every day in the most pristine, well-tailored suit. Flint's collection was made up of suits from Rome to London, England.

Each and every one Flint's suits were customized to his exact fit. For Flint, nothing else was acceptable.

In a life that provided him little joy, Flint's tailored suits gave him at least a little something to feel good about.

Even Flint's beard was a work of well-maintained art. It was always perfectly trimmed, dark brown with a smattering of white flecks.

'Jesus. I do not need this shit,' Flint said, banging his fist onto the desk as his computer crashed yet again. 'When the hell is the mayor going to give us a budget we can actually work with? This computer would have been out of date ten years ago.'

No one responded to Flint.

The other cops were just as over-worked and grouchy as he was.

This was nothing more than a typical day in the department.

Too much work and not enough time to do it.

The heatwave was annoying for more than just its

impact in the office. It was a long held statistical fact that crime went up during heatwaves.

The added heat just made people take risks.

Act out of character. Let their demons take charge and override their good sense.

This meant more work for cops.

Of course, it could have been different.

Rather than spending his days in the pit with the rest of the working detectives, Flint could have been in upper management.

All of his early career success had seen him marked out as a potential leader in the force. The higher-ups had offered him promotion after promotion.

But Flint had turned them down.

Each and every time, Flint's answer was the same. *Thank you, but no.*

Flint had never wanted to live a cushy office-based life. Sure, he would have been earning a much higher salary. And it would be a job with way fewer personal risks or threats to his life.

But that wasn't why Flint had signed up.

He wanted to do proper police work.

On the street level.

Catching and putting the bad guys away.

Speaking of bosses...

'Maddox! In my office, now!' Sergeant Mase bellowed.

Flint got up from his desk and took the short walk over to Sergeant Mase's office.

'Yes, Sir?' Flint said, taking a seat.

Flint had been in this position before. He could sense when he was about to take two full barrels of anger from his boss.

'You're too damned slow!' Mase shouted, pacing up and

down. 'I've got targets to meet. And the time you spend on even the most basic of open and shut cases is getting out of hand.'

'I'm being thorough is all,' Flint replied, trying not to sound annoyed. 'Each case has to be concluded properly. The public must trust us and know we're doing our best for them.'

'All the same, the amount of time you're taking is fucking bananas,' Mase continued. 'You have to speed that ass up. I'm not far off retirement and I'll be damned if you push me into an early grave. Not every case needs the full Flint Maddox investigation. Just get your work done. Process it. Move on. It's not hard.'

'Sir, I appreciate what you're saying,' Flint countered, trying to sound as respectful as he could. 'But I need to disagree. I will give my best to every single case. It's the only way I know how to be a good detective.'

Mase rolled his eyes.

Standing with his hands on his hips, the frustration in Sergeant Mase's face was evident. He could be very grouchy and blunt himself. He was known for it. But beneath it all, there was definitely a good cop there. Maybe even a little heart of gold too.

'Listen, Flint. We go way back,' Mase said, taking a seat. 'I know you struggled after what happened with your partner. It was tough. I've been there. I know how it feels. Trust me on that. But I'm speaking to you as a friend. Your work hasn't been as good since Mickie passed. It's not just the speed you're working at. You just don't have that same focus. Help me out here, man.'

Flint could feel himself getting annoyed.

He didn't like how Mase was speaking to him.

The implication that he wasn't a good cop hurt Flint.

Stung him *bad*.

But Mase wasn't finished yet.

'I think you should consider taking some time off,' Mase said. 'Take a step back for a minute. See how that feels.'

'Respectfully, sir, there's no chance,' Flint barked. 'Now if you'll excuse me, I have some work to be getting on with. At my own pace. And with one goal in mind... keeping the citizens of this city safe.'

Mase tutted and turned away from Flint.

Flint got up from his chair and walked out of the office.

Flint took a quick detour to the water dispenser and poured himself a cup. He downed it in one and immediately refilled.

Flint was furious.

The suggestion that he should take time off had not gone down well at all. It felt like an insult.

Flint prided himself on how good a cop he was.

It was his lifeblood.

There was no way in hell he was taking time off.

If anything, all Mase's words had done was motivate him to take more work on.

Come in early.

Leave later.

The whole nine yards.

Flint took a second however and thought back to his old partner. To what could have been between them. Maybe Mase had a point. Maybe his partner's death had changed him.

It certainly affected Flint's personal life.

Any idea of a relationship seemed crazy.

Flint saw himself as damaged goods now. The emotional hurt he had experienced with his partner had left the kind of scars that would probably never heal.

The hours Flint put into his work meant that he didn't have the time to deal with a Little in his life. Not only that, but he didn't think he was well adjusted enough to handle being a Daddy.

If Flint couldn't give a Little the same amount of care and attention that he gave his case files, then it was a non-starter.

On this basis, Flint had decided that any kind of romantic involvements were pretty much out of the question for him.

He was married to the job.

That was it.

Nothing more, nothing less.

It didn't mean that Flint still didn't have his own kinks and desires.

Of course he did.

But Flint had the discipline to keep them locked away.

That was the only way.

'Flint, those papers still haven't arrived,' Kaplinksi hollered, shrugging his shoulders in frustration. 'It's a cop's life, eh?'

Flint nodded his head in solidarity.

It was frustrating, but all part of the job.

Feeling a little calmer, and with the files he needed still not ready, Flint headed towards the reception to see if there were any new cases he could pick up.

This was something that Sergeant Mase frowned upon.

It was his belief that the detectives should finish their caseloads and wait for the juniors to bring through the new files. That way, Mase could choose who got what.

Flint always wanted to choose himself though.

This was an old trick he picked up from his father.

This way, he could lay claim to the juiciest cases.

But on his arrival in the reception area, Flint had to take a backward step.

Who in New York City's name is that...?

Flint took a moment to compose himself.

At the reception desk was just about the cutest, most gorgeous guy he'd ever seen.

Slender.

Incredible cheekbones.

Perfect big lips and a tight body too.

Flint felt his Daddy-senses going into overload.

He had to get a grip on himself.

This was a professional environment.

He was in a position of power.

This young man looked upset.

Fragile and on the verge of tears.

It was time for Flint to put his best foot forward and show this young guy that he was safe. In good hands. That whatever his problem was, Flint could handle it.

'Sir, Detective Flint Maddox, at your service,' Flint said. 'I'm here to help you. Tell me everything...'

Chapter Three

Who the hell is this approaching me?

Gulp. He's... scary.

But also... totally hot.

Dylan was totally stuck for words when Flint approached him in the reception area of the police station. He wasn't used to being in places like this. Dylan liked to live a fun and passionate life. But one that stayed within the limits of the law.

As such, he had never felt the need to be in a police station.

Until now.

After receiving the super-creepy photo in the mail, Dylan panicked. It was the scariest thing that had ever happened to him. And that included the time he went down the notorious Devil's Canyon slide at his childhood water park.

No, this was deadly serious.

The photo had invaded Dylan's privacy in a way that he just couldn't accept. There was no way he was letting it slide. Even if it was a one off, it was too much.

Way beyond any kind of normal sense of decency.

For all Dylan knew, the culprit could have been his landlord.

It could have been someone who knew him who harbored a grudge.

it could have been a total stranger.

The possibilities were limitless.

And that was what made it so terrifying.

Dylan had no control. No comprehension.

There wasn't even a note with the photo, so it was impossible to even try and guess what the person who sent it wanted from him.

It could have been nothing.

It could have been a badly judged joke or prank.

But Dylan was definitely not risking anything.

That was why he just had to come to the police station to get some kind of grip on things.

'Kid, *hello*? My name is Detective Maddox. Flint Maddox. I'm busy here. What's your issue?' Flint said, tapping the large old watch on his wrist impatiently. 'Young man?'

There was something about the stern authority in Flint's voice that made Dylan tingle all over.

Yes, this was a scary situation.,

But that didn't mean Dylan was entirely unresponsive to hot men.

And in this case, *ridiculously* hot men.

Like, hotter than the surface of the sun levels of hotness.

'Um, I, um, well, it's kinda like this,' Dylan spluttered, his brain not engaging into gear properly. 'I had this photo. I mean, it's not mine. Well, it's *of* me. I mean...'

Dylan gave up.

He felt humiliated and embarrassed at not being able to

get his words out. He wasn't great a pressurized situations. Especially ones that involved authority.

This situation was ticking every bad box that Dylan could imagine.

It was at this point that Flint stepped in.

'Okay, relax, I've got you,' Flint said, placing his large hand on Dylan's slender shoulder. 'Come with me. We'll talk somewhere quieter. Just the two of us. How does that sound?'

Dylan felt reassured.

He also felt his heart beating.

And his dick hardening a little bit too.

Flint was built like a super-human. He looked perfectly smart, like he knew exactly what he was all about it and wasn't afraid of dressing to his exact preference.

That was the thing with older men.

Confidence and experience.

It was a strong vibe.

It was something that Dylan had always found attractive.

A *major* turn-on.

'Okay, yeah, I'd like that,' Dylan said, cringing a little bit about how high pitched his voice went. Especially in comparison to Flint's masculine, rugged baritone voice.

Flint nodded.

There had been no sign of a smile yet.

Not even close.

'Okay, no time to waste,' Flint said. 'Follow me. Now.'

Dylan took a seat in the sparsely furnished private interview room. It wasn't exactly luxury, but at least the aircon was working better than it did in his stuffy apartment.

He felt nervous.

It was strange to be in a police interview room. It looked similar to the kind Dylan saw on TV and in movies.

Grey seats.

Off-white walls.

A square, black desk.

And not much else.

'Okay, talk me through it,' Flint said, taking a seat opposite Dylan. 'There's no rush. I like to take my time. Get the info. Then we'll see what we can do about it all. Okay. When you're ready.'

Dylan took a deep breath.

But there was something reassuring about Flint's masculine authority. He was clearly a well-trained and seasoned professional. That much was clear to Dylan.

What was also increasingly obvious was the sheer scale of Flint's good looks.

It was actually proving difficult for Dylan to focus.

In the end, Dylan shut his eyes so that he could concentrate on the details of the situation without being distracted by Flint's square jaw and perfectly maintained beard.

'I'm... I'm a cam performer,' Dylan said, blushing as the words began to tumble out of his mouth. 'I do shows, perform... *acts*. It's just a way of paying the bills.'

'Okay, go on,' Flint said, no emotion in his voice.

'Some of the stuff I do is quite naughty,' Dylan continued, unable to stop his cheeks continuing to burn hard with embarrassment. 'But it's all legal. The thing is... I got this photo sent to me and...'

At this point, Dylan began to struggle to speak again.

The memory of receiving the photo was still fresh.

Too fresh.

He had to compose himself to carry on. Flint handed him a small cup of ice-cold water. The water helped. As

Dylan continued to explain what had happened with the photo, he could see that Flint was paying close attention to what he was saying.

Flint cared.

Dylan could see that clearly.

'I didn't even want to do the cam shows,' Dylan said, taking a brief sidetrack from the story. 'My real passion is theatre. That's what I came to New York for. Anyway. Hasn't quite worked out like that for me yet.'

Flint continued to listen.

He would take the odd note, but for the most part he kept his gaze firmly on Dylan. His eyes seemed caring, but there was no getting away from the fact that for the most part he seemed... very serious.

Like, *seriously* serious.

Dylan was a Little and as such his life was all about being upbeat, having fun, and laughing as much as possible. He hadn't seen Flint smile once this whole time.

Maybe that was understandable.

After all, he was a police detective.

And this was a serious situation of course.

'Okay, I think that's everything,' Dylan said. 'Phew. It actually feels a little better to have got it off my chest.'

Flint stood up from this chair and paced around the room.

Dylan tried to read his reaction.

Was Flint excited by Dylan's mentioning of being a theatre performer? Was that something that could possibly appeal to him?

No, he'd just think it was silly.

I'm way too much of a Little for a big serious man like Flint...

But as much as Dylan doubted that Flint would be into

him, he also couldn't deny that he was picking up some Daddy-vibes.

Flint was a big, rock-solid figure of a man.

He was stern. Serious.

His voice sounded gruff and had a hint of someone who could dish out a punishment or several - and almost certainly enjoy it too.

These factors were all very much in the wheelhouse for a Daddy.

But Dylan was still trying to guess if Flint was potentially a Daddy or not when Flint brought the interview to an abrupt end.

'Kid, there's not much we can do,' Flint said, his voice hinting at emotion. 'I'm sorry. The law is the law. I want to help you more. Of course. But right now, this is all we can do.'

Dylan felt sad.

This wasn't what he hoped for.

By the emotion in Flint's voice, Dylan could tell that this wasn't the ideal outcome for him either.

'B-b-b-but there must be something you can do?' Dylan said, the reality hitting home. 'Maybe a bodyguard?'

The reality hit home *hard* in fact.

Dylan felt vulnerable and scared.

What if someone sent another photograph?

'You've been watching too many Hollywood movies, young man,' Flint said, chuckling slightly at Dylan's suggestion. 'But here, take this.'

Flint took a card out of his jacket pocket and handed it to Dylan.

It was Flint's detective calling card, complete with his office and cell phone details.

'If anything else happens, call me,' Flint said. 'And I

mean anything at all. Seriously. I'm at the other end of the phone. Waiting. Ready to be there for you.'

Dylan blushed and took the card from Flint.

The interview was over.

Yet somehow Dylan left the police station with even more questions than he had arrived with...

* * *

Dylan arrived back at his apartment none the wiser.

Yes, Flint had been very attentive and seemed to take Dylan's problem seriously. But he had also said that there was nothing that could be done at the moment.

That hadn't been the outcome Dylan had wanted.

Far from it.

Come to think of it, the way Flint had laughed at his suggestion of a bodyguard really wasn't very nice.

Dylan walked over towards his refrigerator and took out a small carton of apple and kiwi juice. He popped the straw into the carton and took a long gulp.

It was still *so hot* in his apartment.

Even with the refurbished aircon, there was no escaping the sheer intensity of the heat.

Dylan walked over toward the window and listened to the sound of the car horns beeping down below.

It scared Dylan to think that someone could be watching him at that very moment. To not feel entirely comfortable in his own apartment was a horrible thing to experience.

A bodyguard wasn't such a crazy idea.

The more he thought about it, the more annoyed Dylan got.

His problem was real.

He deserved to be looked after.

'If someone was spying on you, I'd definitely be your bodyguard!' Dylan said, walking over toward Pinky, his stuffie. 'Not like that big stinky-pants cop laughing at me!'

One thing was puzzling Dylan.

He knew that he felt attracted to Flint. How could he not? He was super-hot. An absolute hunk of a man.

But Dylan wondered if Flint felt an attraction to him.

There had *definitely* been hints.

During the interview, Dylan had caught Flint's eyes wandering over his body once or twice. Sizing him up. Almost licking his lips at one point.

And there was the way that for the most part Flint seemed genuinely invested in Dylan's problem. Like more than he would have been with another person maybe.

It was so hard to tell.

After all, it was definitely a possibility that Flint was just doing his job and taking a close interest in the civilian who had entered his station with a problem.

Urgh. Maybe I should call Casper and see what he thinks?

No, Casper's probably busy on his webcomic. I don't want to disturb him.

I wish I knew what to think.

Dylan figured in that moment that it was pointless even wondering whether Flint was a Daddy or not. No matter how good-looking Dylan found him, things could never possibly work out between a police detective and a cam boy.

No chance.

Never.

Not in a million, billion years.

So instead of calling Flint to check in, Dylan took his

card and tore it up into pieces and dropped them on the floor beneath him.

'I'll clean it up later, Pinky, okay?' Dylan said to his loyal stuffie.

Then, in one last attempt to relax, Dylan picked up his Kindle and sat down to carry on reading his latest romance novel. This was the only way he knew how to truly relax.

There was something about losing himself in a good book that managed to switch Dylan off from the outside world.

Similar to his love of theatre, it was an escape into a fantasy world that appealed.

There was comfort for Dylan in knowing that the romance novels he read came with guaranteed happily ever afters. There would be ups and downs along the way, but things would always work out for the best in the end.

The only question was whether Dylan's actual life would have a guaranteed happily ever after. In that moment, the answer looked like it could go either way.

Chapter Four

The evening air was hot and humid.

The streetlights were on full beam, their light radiating across the sidewalk and illuminating people's hot and sweaty faces as they went about their business.

Flint had taken a big drink of water before he left his apartment. The glass had been full of ice cubes too. But it made little difference by this stage.

Flint was hot with a capital H.

A glass of iced water wasn't much competition to a city-wide heatwave that was going to go down in the record books as one for the ages.

Flint's crisp white t-shirt was beginning to cling to his body. He needed to get to the bar and its all-out aircon as a matter of urgency.

But he was still three blocks away.

This was not great.

As he continued to walk, Flint heard his phone buzzing in his pocket. Stopping briefly, he took the handset out of his tight blue denim jeans and looked.

A message from his friend, Jackson.

· · ·

Yo, Flint! You nearly here? It's my round. I'll grab you a bottle. Luther's already arrived of course. Move that cop ass of yours. Double quick time! Jackson.

Flint rolled his eyes. Jackson was a real stickler for time-keeping. It was one of his things.

Flint wasn't even late.

He had planned the departure from his apartment perfectly.

Oh well, there was no pleasing some people.

The knowledge that there was a beer ready and waiting for him *was* good motivation to walk faster, however.

Flint couldn't deny that.

Above everything else, Flint truly valued the fact that he had such good friends as Jackson and Luther. They had known each other for quite some time by this point.

Their friendships had been tested.

Ups and downs.

Stresses and strains.

But the one thing that had never come into question had been the true strength of the bond between each one of them.

Together, they were quite a formidable unit.

With this in mind, and despite the sweltering heat, Flint broke out of his walk and into a jog.

It was time to hit the bar and sink some brewskis.

'Hey! Look who decided to show!' Jackson said, his larger-than-life voice crashing across the bar. 'I would have bet my last buck on you getting here late. But this is crazy!'

'Enough. Relax, I'm here!' Flint said, a broad smile on his face as he embraced Jackson and Luther one after the other.

The three amigos were reunited.

It felt great.

Jackson immediately continued with a story. Something about a cute guy he had helped earlier that day.

Jackson was a firefighter.

Meeting cute guys seemed to happen to him on a daily basis.

This wasn't much of a surprise.

Even taking out the raw appeal of being a firefighter, Jackson had the kind of extremely masculine face that younger guys seemed to love.

His twin dimples on his cheeks were an unexpected bonus.

People went *wild* for them.

Other than this, Jackson had the warm brown eyes and storytelling swagger that perfectly matched his wild yet caring personality.

He enjoyed gambling too.

As far as Jackson was concerned, there was no bet he didn't think he could find an angle on and win.

Maybe this was a strength.

Maybe it was a weakness.

Either way, it made him great fun to be around.

'So, you going to call this guy?' Flint said.

'*Nah*. I don't know. Maybe, maybe not,' Jackson said, shrugging his shoulders. 'I'm busy. You know? Same old, same old.'

Flint suspected he knew what Jackson was talking about, but before he could ask, Luther cut in.

'Guys, we need to do our toast!' Luther said, his green eyes seeming to sparkle even more than normal. As an emergency ER doctor, he had had yet another busy day and was now in the mood to unwind. 'Even you Mr. Serious!'

Luther was talking to Flint.

'I'm down to toast, don't worry,' Flint said, raising his glass. 'One... two... three... Here's to *The Hero Daddies*!'

The three of them toasted and took long gulps on their beers.

The name Hero Daddies was a kind of joke name they called their group. Each one of the men was a Daddy Dom and they also each worked in one form of the emergency services.

Flint was a cop.

Jackson a firefighter.

Luther an ER doctor.

They'd all met at a Little Club in the city and yet to this day none of them had Littles in their lives. It may have been a combination of how busy their lives were and past dramas that made this the way. It wasn't ideal. Certainly, each would have liked their own forever Little to call their own.

Whatever.

It didn't affect their bond as a three.

Three Daddy Doms who enjoyed hanging together and shooting the shit over a few cold beers.

It was *perfect*.

After the toast, normal service was resumed.

It was time for Jackson to tell the tale of another one of his stories. As well as being a firefighter, Jackson was something of a computer whizz.

In fact, he was a white hat hacker.

This was a hacker who didn't set out to steal from people or cause trouble to private individuals who had done nothing wrong. No, a white hat hacker was someone who sought to hack for good ethical reasons and causes.

And Jackson was pretty damn skilled in this field.

'You know, I was a click away,' Jackson said. 'A single click away from the money reserve in the state department budget. I could have moved it all to some offshore account and retired to a secret island somewhere. Of course, what I actually did was contact that state and tell them that they needed to boost their security.'

'Weren't you tempted?' Luther said, a big smile on his face. 'Just imagine how much money you could bet. Gambling from your own private beach too!'

The three men laughed.

Sure, there was temptation in life. But they had each chosen a life of public service and they loved it. None of them would have change it for anything.

The beers continued to flow, and the three Hero Daddies took turns playing each other at pool.

Luther was pretty decent.

Probably the strongest player.

His favorite way to relax during Med School had been to shoot pool at a local bar. Luther found it relaxing while at the same time gave him an excuse to let his perfectionist streak come out.

Luther always wanted to play the perfect game.

This wasn't always possible of course.

But it didn't stop Luther getting annoyed when he missed a shot.

'Jesus!' Luther bellowed as the yellow ball cannoned off the cushion and missed the hole by mere millimeters. 'That was the beer. I'm better than that.'

'Chill,' Flint said. 'There are worse situations in life than missing the occasional easy shot in pool. Trust me. I see them every day.'

'You think I don't know that?' Luther retorted. 'I work in the ER of the city's busiest hospital. I see things every shift that would make the toughest guy go weak at the knees with horror.'

'Okay, okay, I think it's fair to say that we all know how tough life is,' Jackson said, laughing as he took the heat out of the moment. 'Moving on. What's new with you Flint? Seen anyone who takes your fancy recently?'

Flint shrugged and took his shot.

He wasn't giving anything away.

And as a detective with many years of experience he felt sure that if any one of the three of them knew how to keep a secret, it was him.

But what he hadn't counted on was Jackson's hacker's intuition.

'Hmmm, I'm not buying it,' Jackson said, placing his hand on the pool table's green felted surface. 'My senses tell me that this Daddy Dom has his eyes on someone. Tell me I'm wrong.'

At this point, the heat was very much on Flint.

Both Jackson and Luther stared at him with serious intent.

They knew Flint was holding something back.

It was only a matter of time before he cracked...

'Urgh. What the hell. You guys always get me to talk in the end,' Flint said. 'Yeah. Okay. There's a guy. A very cute guy in fact.'

Luther and Jackson high-fived.

They were pleased to have out-copped the cop.

'His name's Dylan. He's super cute, very sexy,' Flint

said, his mind all over the place thinking about Dylan. 'Great body. Incredible face too. He's sweet. But...'

There was a pause.

Flint wasn't sure how much he should say.

He reminded himself to be professional.

It was his duty as an officer of the law to respect and maintain Dylan's privacy.

'Well, I can't go into any specifics of course, but he came into the station with a problem,' Flint said. 'Hard to say how serious. Could be nothing. Could be something. Either way, I haven't been able to get him out of my head. At all. I mean, you know those late-night moments, lying alone in bed...'

'Yup, I hear that,' Luther laughed.

'Same,' Jackson added. 'So, you going to reach out to this dude or what?'

'It's not just that I think he's hot though,' Flint said. 'I do have a sense that he's not entirely safe. A hunch. I'm not often wrong when my instincts kick in. Police work is in my DNA.'

Flint's two friends nodded in solidarity.

They could see that he was taking this seriously.

'I'm almost certain he's a Little, too,' Flint continued. 'He's the kind of young guy who needs protecting. He's vulnerable. I can tell. Needs a man to be his protector. This is a big, scary city at times. Littles need that guiding voice and protecting hand over their shoulder. Right?'

'Agreed,' Jackson and Luther said simultaneously.

Despite none of them having their own Littles, each one of the three Hero Daddies knew the importance of making sure that Littles were safe and well looked after.

Even if that meant administering some discipline from time to time.

Hell, that could even be the most fun part!

Luther took the needs of Littles very seriously. With Luther being a doctor, patient care was a big priority for him. As such, he had spent a lot of time learning about how different people have different needs unique to them. Littles were a group of people who typically needed a lot of reassurance, guidance, care and attention.

Luther stroked his big beard and flexed his huge arms.

He was deep in thought.

'Hey, what's the worst that could happen? A serial killer specializing in Littles?' Luther laughed.

Jackson and Flint rolled their eyes.

Luther had a wicked sense of humor.

Typical with his at times gallows humor, Luther could go to some dark places.

But it was only because he cared so much.

'Y'all know I'm joking,' Luther said, arching his eyebrow. 'I think you know what you need to do, my dude.'

Luther smiled reassuringly at Flint.

'I've got a lot to think about,' Flint said, his mind already beginning to do some calculations.

But before he got too deep into Dylan's situation, there was the small matter of finishing off the game of pool and then getting the next round of cold ones in.

After a few more games of pool, and a large glass of iced water to round the night off, Flint headed back in the direction of his apartment.

The night air was cooling down now.

It was a welcome respite from the suffocating evening heat.

35

All of the usual sights and sounds of nighttime were around Flint.

Street vendors selling their late-night snacks.

Couples walking happily, and sometimes *not so happily,* home.

Groups of friends enjoying their nights together.

Each and every citizen was on a different journey with a different outcome. It was what made the big city so compelling to live in.

No two individuals were the same.

Everyone had a story to tell.

Flint thought back to his first day on the streets as a beat cop. It was many years ago now, but his passion for helping people had not wavered. Even taking into account what had happened with his partner, Flint knew that the thing that drove him on in life was the knowledge that he could be of assistance.

The only problem was that there were so many people who needed help. Flint knew from experience that it was better not to over-think this.

All he could do was work with the tools he had been given.

One problem at a time.

It took a police siren in the distance to focus Flint's mind.

I must do it. I know it's a risk. But I just have to cross this line...

Before he could consider what he was about to do any further, Flint took his cellphone out and called the station.

He had to find out where Dylan lived.

Flint may have been crossing a line, but deep down he felt utterly convinced it was the right option.

The *only* option.

Flint had to make sure that Dylan was okay.

If he was in any danger whatsoever, then it was his duty to look after him and keep Dylan from harm's way.

It was his duty as a cop.

And it was his duty as a potential Daddy too.

Chapter Five

Sometimes the answer to stress was to have fun.

There was simply no other option.

Despite everything that was going on, Dylan knew that he had to try and put a positive spin on things. And who better to do that with than his friend Casper?

As well as writing a popular DDlb webcomic, Casper was also interested in acting and singing.

Just like Dylan.

The pair of them met at an audition and had been best pals ever since. It was like they shared a connection that ran way beyond both of them being Littles.

It was almost like they were brothers.

With his bright blue eyes and peroxide blonde hair, Casper stood out from the crowd. He was always gaining admiring glances from Daddies and Doms when the pair of them were out partying.

Casper was creative, thoughtful and had a superb sense of humor too. He was always making Dylan laugh. It was like he knew exactly what to say and how to say it too.

Casper's comedic gifts came to the fore in his webcomic.

Dylan would eagerly wait for the latest edition to drop on Casper's Patreon and devour it on one sitting. Often, he would re-read it immediately to pick up on some of the jokes and gags he might have missed on the first read-through.

Dylan felt honored to have such a talented friend.

Casper always supported Dylan in his own creative endeavors too. After every audition, Casper was always there to provide support and feedback. He was convinced that Dylan would make it on Broadway one day, even if Dylan's faith in himself had dipped in recent times.

Tonight was no different.

Casper was in great form.

The laughs hadn't stopped since the second he had entered through the door.

The pair of them were putting on a late-night performance of *Romeo and Juliet* using stuffies.

This was *classic* Casper.

He always knew how to put an amusing spin on an old classic. His webcomic was known for its parodies of grand old movies and plays.

Plus, the opportunity to break out Dylan's complete stuffie collection was too good to miss.

'This will be the greatest show on earth!' Casper declared as he held aloft his own stuffie, Micah. The lop-eared neon green bunny waved from side to side as Casper lifted the makeshift curtain to reveal the cast of characters.

In this version of the classic Shakespearean play, a teddy bear actor called Roman and a bunny rabbit police officer called Julio were deeply in love.

The stuffies' bond was despite their contrasting back-grounds and personalities.

Dylan and Casper had built an elaborate set using duvet covers, cardboard, balloons and a variety of colorful pillows.

It looked *superb*.

It was the kind of guaranteed fun and wholesome activity that would help Dylan relax. Get him closer to finding his Little Space. This was when any Little felt at their most natural.

Happiest.

Free to behave exactly how they most wanted to without fear of judgement.

With Casper alongside him and their entire cast of stuffie characters, everything was looking good.

'Hey, it's good to see you smiling again,' Casper said, picking up an elephant stuffie and placing him back on the stage. 'You've had my back often enough. I had to make sure you were okay. Figured this would be a good idea.'

'It super-duper definitely one million percent was a good idea!' Dylan squealed, joyfully helping Roman the stuffie across the stage. 'I owe you one!'

Before Dylan could continue with the play, there was a loud knocking at the door.

Dylan froze.

Panic surged over his body.

Who was knocking so late?

Dylan wasn't expecting anyone.

It could be his sleazy landlord.

Yuck.

Or worse, it could be the creep who had sent him the photo.

That was *even worse*.

'Aren't you going to answer that?' Casper said. 'It could be an Amazon delivery? Remember that new coloring set you ordered?'

'*Hmm*, I guess,' Dylan said, a little unsure.

Dylan got to his feet and walked over towards the door.

He took a deep breath and just before he opened the door, a voice came through from the other side.

'It's me, Detective Maddox. I've come to check in on you, Dylan.'

OMG.

This is... kinda strange.

But I'm super-excited too...

Dylan opened the door and immediately felt himself get excited by the sight of Flint standing there in his doorway.

Flint was so tall and handsome.

Even in more casual clothing he looked incredible.

Flint was the hottest off-duty cop Dylan had ever seen.

'Please, come in,' Dylan said, stepping to one side and pointing Flint inside the apartment.

'I was just in the area,' Flint said, standing in the middle of the living space, casting his eyes over the room. 'I thought it would be a good idea to stop by. See that everything was okay with you. You know, after you came into the station.'

Dylan nodded in thanks.

After a quick but excited exchange of looks with Dylan, Casper made an exit.

Dylan knew that Casper would be messaging him frantically later on.

But right now, it was time to focus his thoughts on Flint.

'Cute toys,' Flint said, pointing over towards the stuffies. 'Looks like you were having a fun time. That's good. You can't allow yourself to live in fear.'

Dylan appreciated the way Flint was so understanding and accepting of the stuffies.

Not all men would be.

Some people could be very judgmental and react badly to seeing something like this.

Dylan knew that from painful experience.

But Flint was showing himself to be different.

Very different.

Dylan continued to watch as Flint wandered around the apartment. Flint was checking the windows. Running his strong hands across the window ledges. Seeing what was up.

'You could do with some better window locks,' Flint said, the professional and serious tone back in his voice. 'The door too. I can help fix that.'

'Y-y-y-yes, thank you,' Dylan said, nervously.

'So, that other guy?' Flint enquired, running his hand up and down the front door. 'Is he your boyfriend?'

'Casper?' Dylan exclaimed, almost bursting out into laughter. 'No, he's not my type! He's great. I love him. But we're BFFs, nothing else.'

Flint grunted a response as he continued to check underneath ledges. Based on what Dylan had seen on TV and in movies, it was possible Flint was checking for bugs or secret recording devices.

Dylan was too scared to ask about that.

He almost would rather not know if that was the case.

'Those window locks you mentioned, are they... expensive?' Dylan asked, knowing full well that he couldn't afford to spend money on extra home security. 'I'm not exactly rolling in dollars at the moment.'

Dylan sighed.

It sucked to not have money.

Especially when it meant that he wasn't even able to afford to make himself more secure at home.

Flint could evidently see that Dylan was a little bit down.

'Hey, I've got an idea,' Flint said, stopping his checks and walking over to Dylan. 'If you feel scared, *seriously* scared, and if you haven't got anywhere else to stay... then come and live with me.'

Did I just hear that right?

Dylan didn't know what to stay.

He was speechless.

His mouth was so wide open he could have taken in the most super-sized sub available in the city.

On the one hand, it sounded like something Dylan might have read in one of his romance novels.

A hot, hunky and domineering cop takes in a soft, sensitive Little.

It was the stuff dreams are made of.

But Dylan had to be realistic.

It would just lead to so many possible complications.

Plus, as Flint himself had said, there was no way he should live his life in fear of some external threat.

Anyway, there might not be any more photos.

It could have been a horrible one-off.

'Thank you for the offer, but no,' Dylan blurted out, still not entirely sure if this was the right thing to do. 'I don't mean it as an insult, but-'

'No, no, it's fine,' Flint said, his tone even.

If Flint was offended or upset at having his offer turned down, he sure was hiding it well.

The pair of them continued to talk about more DIY security improvements that Dylan could make. Changes and fixes that wouldn't impact on Dylan's limited budget.

Dylan thought that Flint was being very kind.

Part of him wanted to ask Flint to stay longer.

But Dylan knew that it could lead to their attraction boiling over into something else. Something *way* more complex.

Also, Dylan just couldn't bring himself to ask Flint to stay. He actually felt a bit weird having someone in his apartment that he didn't know well.

Casper was a totally different case.

They were longtime friends and the trust had been established.

But Flint was different.

Even though he did seem a decent and honorable man, and was hot as anything on top of that, Dylan just didn't know him.

Eventually, the conversation came to a standstill and Flint left.

'Remember, I'm at the other end of the line if you need me,' Flint said, his warm eyes and sincere tone making Dylan feel hot and tingly inside.

Dylan smiled and slowly shut the door.

He watched as Flint powered down the corridor. His stride was long. He walked with certainty. Flint was a serious man who undertook serious business.

Sigh.

Back to being on my lonesome.

At least I have my stuffies and novels to keep me company...

With the door fully shut, Dylan headed into his bedroom and stripped down ready for bed.

He could have stayed up later.

Maybe watched a movie.

But he knew that what he actually needed was a good

night's sleep.

Things would look different in the morning.

They always did.

After managing only a single chapter of his latest novel, Dylan's eyes began to shut. The cozy duvet was wrapped around his body and Pinky was tucked up under his arm.

Even thoughts of Flint in various stages of undress couldn't keep Dylan awake.

Before he knew it, he was fast asleep.

* * *

Dylan woke in the morning and right away something felt *off*.

There was a strange vibe in the bedroom.

Dylan couldn't quite put his finger on it, but he felt scared.

Immediately, he reached over the side of the bed and pulled up a pair of pants to put on.

Despite his increasing sense of fear, Dylan got off the bed and walked out in the apartment.

To his horror, the front door was open.

He'd *definitely* locked it the previous night.

Dylan had even triple-checked it.

There was a rising sense of panic coursing over Dylan.

This was like something out of a thriller or horror movie. Dylan knew that someone had been in his apartment while he slept. There was no other explanation for the open door.

But it wasn't a burglar.

It didn't appear that anything had been stolen.

Or even touched.

Then he saw it.

Dylan scurried over to the kitchen table and picked up the polaroid.

It was a photo of him, fast asleep in bed last night.

What the...

I don't like this. This is horrible...

Next to the polaroid was a note that read:

You're even more beautiful in the flesh...

Dylan felt like he wanted to cry.

This was the worst wake-up he had ever experienced in his entire life.

He felt lost and exposed.

More than ever, Dylan felt alone and totally without any control over what was happening to him.

Dylan knew what he had to do.

It was time to call the police and try to sort this out properly.

One cop in particular came to mind.

But after he had rejected Flint's offer the previous night, Dylan wasn't sure whether Flint would be interested in helping anymore.

But now wasn't the time to think too much about his maybe-Daddy crush. Dylan felt like he was in real danger and knew that there was only one realistic course of action he could take.

His hands still shaking from the shock, Dylan picked up his cell phone and dialed 911.

Whether Detective Flint Maddox would show up was uncertain.

But there was only one way to find out.

Chapter Six

'This flight of stairs sure seemed shorter last time,' Flint said gruffly to the beat cop walking with him. 'Maybe I'm getting old? Actually, don't answer that.'

Flint was back at Dylan's apartment building.

As soon as the call came into the station, Flint was all over it.

There was no way anyone else was going to get to lead on this case.

Not a chance in hell, in fact.

Part of Flint was frustrated and annoyed that he hadn't been more insistent with Dylan when it came to the offer he made.

On the other hand, Flint had respected Dylan's decision.

That was a big thing for Flint.

Everyone had the right to make their own mind up and have a say in how their life was. It was part of the reason he was so passionate about his work.

No one should have to feel ashamed or scared to live their best life.

Flint arrived at the apartment door and saw that a couple of forensic officers were there, already working their way around the place.

There was no sight of Dylan.

As Flint began to work over the apartment, he was frustrated that there were no obvious mistakes from the person, or people, who had broken in.

It was someone who knew what they were doing.

Whoever had done this had covered their tracks effectively.

This wasn't ideal.

Flint decided to speak to the landlord.

Maybe he would have some answers.

'Urgh, no? Sorry. Nothing,' the landlord replied when Flint made his enquiry.

Flint shook his head.

'But surely you have some kind of system to log guests in and out?' Flint asked, struggling to hide his disgust at the landlord. 'Come on, what kind of place is this?'

'Nope. Nothing. We're not exactly a five-star experience here, officer.'

'That's *detective* to you,' Flint said, his frustration beginning to boil over. 'How about cleaners? Were any working last night?'

'Could have been,' the landlord smirked. 'But, again, it's outsourced so I wouldn't know. I'm the landlord, not some kind of uber-janitor.'

The landlord was useless. Some people had this kind of naturally off-putting unhelpful vibe and the landlord very much fell into that category.

Not only was the landlord a fat load of help, but he also gave off a sleazy vibe that irritated Flint.

The thought of Dylan having to deal with a guy like this bothered Flint a lot.

Damn it, my Daddy senses need to shut off for a second.

I need to focus on the case.

'Okay, you can go now,' Flint said rather abruptly to the landlord. 'Thanks for all your help.'

The landlord laughed as he walked away, further annoying Flint. It came to something when a landlord wasn't even concerned for the safety of one of his own tenants.

It didn't seem right to Flint.

In fact, it actually seemed weird.

Why wouldn't the landlord want to see his tenants happy and safe? Surely this was the best way to guarantee rent was paid regularly and on time too.

The whole situation was wrong.

'Sir, we're coming up with nothing but blanks here,' the lead forensics officer said. 'I know that's not the answer you want to hear.'

'No, it's fine, thank you for your efforts,' Flint replied. 'We have to play the hand we're dealt. If that means no evidence, then it means we'll solve the case another way.'

Flint was nothing if not determined.

He had been working cases for long enough to know that there would always be a few curve balls thrown in.

No case was the same.

It never was.

Although that didn't stop the same problems raising their heads.

A meeting with the building supervisor confirmed that there was no CCTV footage available.

This was a blow.

The lack of forensics was one thing but having not a

single shred of visual evidence as to who had been coming and going was hard to stomach.

Maybe the landlord actually had a decent point?

Maybe the landlord wasn't wrong when he said that this was the kind of run-down, budget building that really didn't have anything by the way of effective security. It would explain how the perpetrator got in and out without being detected.

There was something here that Flint was missing.

He could sense it.

But *what*?

Before Flint could dwell on it for too long, Dylan walked around the corner.

'Hey, Dylan, how are you?' Flint said, trying to sound as sensitive as his voice would allow. 'I understand this must be a tough moment for you.'

Dylan was visible shaken by the experience.

It was totally understandable.

Dylan's eyes looked red from crying. His perfectly clear skin looked a little blotchy from tears too. It was almost heartbreaking to see.

Less than twenty-four hours ago, Flint had walked in on Dylan acting out a play with his stuffies and his friend.

Dylan had looked so full of life then.

But that was before his privacy was violated for a second time.

It would take a harsh toll on anyone, but the danger wasn't just psychological.

It was physical.

Flint was fearful for Dylan's safety. Living alone was no place for a vulnerable Little in a situation like this.

It was a recipe for disaster.

However, Dylan's rejection of his offer was still fresh in Flint's mind.

There had to be another way.

But before that, Flint knew that they had to set the record straight. Establish exactly what was going on between them.

'Listen, I have an offer to make,' Flint said. 'But first, tell me something. Are you a Little?'

Dylan blushed but then sweetly nodded his head.

It was kind of exciting for Flint.

First and foremost, he was a detective. His duty was undoubtedly to serve.

But he was attracted to Dylan, there was no escaping that.

'Okay, I did have a feeling that was the case,' Flint continued. 'Here's my offer. I know you don't want to move in with me. That's fine. No problem. But at least let me pay for a hotel for you while I arrange for some security experts to get your apartment into shape, totally free of charge. What do you say?'

Flint stood with his hands on his hips.

He could see that Dylan was thinking things over.

Come on kid, it's a golden opportunity.

Just as Flint was beginning to feel impatient, Dylan spoke...

'Thank you so much, but no,' Dylan said, much to Flint's shock.

'Are you being serious?' Flint replied, struggling to keep his frustration in check. 'If it's about the money you can pay me back in installments damn it.'

'Is the other offer still on the table?' Dylan said, shyly.

Flint was confused.

The other offer as in the one that Dylan had already rejected the previous night?

'You make me feel safe,' Dylan said, twiddling his fingers nervously. 'If I'm with you I don't think anything bad could ever happen to me. I want to live with you. If you'll still have me. I promise I'll be good.'

Flint felt a burning desire come over him.

His Daddy energy went into full-on afterburner mode.

Flint felt his dick begin to twitch inside his pure-black Calvin Klein briefs.

But more than just a sexual charge, Flint actually felt like this was an opportunity to do some good.

To help this Little feel safe and secure.

At least until the case was solved.

'Are you looking for a Daddy?' Flint said, knowing that this was the kind of thing they would have to make clear before entering into any kind of living arrangement. 'Be honest.'

'I... I... don't know,' Dylan replied, his voice trembling a little.

'Well, whether you are or not, the offer stands,' Flint replied. 'My duty is to look after you. And that is *exactly* what I will do.'

Flint could see that his words were having a reassuring effect on Dylan.

This was good to see.

In fact, it made Flint glow with pride.

Sure, this was a horrible situation, but that didn't mean that some positives couldn't come out of it.

Even if a relationship between them didn't develop on a Daddy-Little level, then the fact that Flint had protected someone who needed help would be more than enough.

'Okay, but if you really want help, we'll need to agree

upon a few things,' Flint added, a note of stern caution in his voice. 'Deal?'

Dylan smiled coyly and looked up to Flint.

The pair were now standing very close.

There was barely a sheet of paper's worth of distance between the two of them.

Flint's body towered above Dylan's.

There was a moment of brief, pulsating electricity between them.

Flint felt like they were seconds away from kissing.

However, a passing forensic officer put paid to any chance of that happening.

'So?' Flint said, a wry smile on his face. 'Do we have a deal?'

This time, Dylan didn't need to pause for thought.

The answer was already on his lips.

'Yep,' Dylan replied swiftly, his voice soft and sweet. 'We've got a deal.'

Flint allowed himself a brief smile.

But only for a fraction of a second.

Dylan wasn't safe yet.

Not by a long shot.

And all of this wasn't even factoring how Dylan would react to Flint's apartment. It certainly wasn't filled with stuffies or colorful paint sets.

No, Flint's place was an altogether different kettle of fish.

And Dylan was about to find out *exactly* how different.

Chapter Seven

Okay, so this is... different.

Like really-really-super-mega different...

Dylan paused and took a moment to assess his surroundings.

They had arrived at Flint's apartment.

The drive over to Flint's place had been quiet. Flint seemed preoccupied with the case. He hadn't revealed any details, but Dylan could tell that Flint's mind was working overtime.

That said, it had felt good to be in the Uber with Flint.

Safe.

Secure.

A totally different sensation to how it felt back at Dylan's apartment. That place was less of a home and more of a bad memory. From camming to the photographs. It was bad vibes.

Despite the lack of talking in the Uber, Dylan had felt comfortable in Flint's company. Sure, he barely knew Flint. But there was something there between them.

A connection.

Whether it was platonic, or something that could develop into a Daddy and Little relationship wasn't entirely clear.

Everything was up in the air.

But now at Flint's apartment, it was time to see exactly how things would play out.

The building looked very nice from the outside. It was a classic, old-school block. The original features had all been maintained both on the outside building work and on the inner lobby too.

For a moment, Dylan even felt a little bit intimidated by the more upscale surroundings. It was absolutely an upgrade from his own shabby apartment building.

If anything, Flint's place was more like the kind of building that Dylan dreamed about living in.

Of course, he'd need to land more than one Broadway role before he could even think about a place of his own that was comparable.

Either that or work a billion hours camming.

Yuck.

The elevator up to Flint's apartment was smooth and even had the old-timey brass buttons to choose the floor. Dylan imagined himself going up and down on the elevator all day, the pinging noises on each floor sounding like something from the musicals he would obsess over as a child growing up.

Inside Flint's apartment was no less impressive.

The only problem was that it didn't seem like the kind of place a Little would live.

At all.

Everything about Flint's home was so grown up compared to Dylan's place.

The furniture was sleek, minimalist.

Classy and expensive too.

The oak flooring was super-shiny and looked like it had only recently been polished.

The furniture was all dark or muted tones. Although Dylan had to admit that the enormous couch did look amazingly comfortable.

Oh, and the huge flat screen TV mounted on the wall was impressive as well.

Beneath the TV was a large, and extremely realistic, electric fireplace. Dylan's mind immediately projected forward to cozy nights in watching a movie and snuggling up as the fire emanated golden waves of heat.

Maybe Flint's place isn't so bad after all...

'Fancy a cup of warm milk?' Flint said, walking over to his kitchen area and opening the large refrigerator door. 'I could make you a warm oat milk with chocolate sprinkles?'

Dylan was a little bit taken aback.

The drink sounded delicious.

Exactly the kind of thing he would love.

But Dylan hadn't expected Flint to be tuned in to his needs like this.

'Yes, I'd love that!' Dylan replied, keen to sound enthusiastic to show his appreciation. 'I love warm milk, especially with extras on top!'

Flint nodded and started to prepare the drink.

Dylan couldn't help but stare in admiration at Flint's body.

It wasn't long before that admiration turned to something else.

Lust.

It was hard to deny that Flint wasn't pretty much the sexiest guy Dylan had ever been in close proximity to.

He was *really* hot.

56

Pretty much the exact physical specification that any Little would describe as being in the Dream Daddy mode.

And here Flint was, making Dylan his very own warm milk with sprinkles.

It was almost too good to be true.

'Here you go, kid. Enjoy,' Flint said, handing Dylan the cup and leading him over to the large kitchen island table where they both sat. 'Let's talk. Tell me about your job.'

Dylan initially felt nervous to speak.

As welcoming as Flint was, he was still very intimidating.

But gradually, Dylan loosened up and was able to say more.

'The thing with camming is that in theory you choose how much you reveal, or what you do,' Dylan said. 'But if you want to earn more money you have do more extreme things. I'm not judging anyone who does, but I'm not always comfortable. Sometime though I just feel like I have to push myself a bit further. And then when my landlord told me about the upcoming rent increases. *Urgh.* Let's just say I'm not exactly in love with the job.'

Flint listened.

There was a calm, non-judgmental look on his face.

Dylan could tell that he was listening with an open mind.

'Have you ever had any trouble like this before?' Flint asked, his clear and controlled way of speaking putting Dylan at ease.

Dylan knew he could trust Flint.

And trust was extremely important.

'No, not really,' Dylan replied. 'I guess I've been lucky. Or was up to this point anyway. It really scared me. I just... didn't know that anything like this was possible. I mean, I've heard of other cam boys getting over-enthusiastic fans. But this is just next level. Thank you again so much for helping like this.'

'Don't mention it, kid,' Flint said, glugging down the last of his drink. 'Hey, this was tasty. I'm not sure if I'll convert from strong black coffee though.'

Dylan giggled.

There was a spot of cream on Flint's lip.

Dylan pointed with his finger and laughed as Flint took a moment to realize what was up.

'As I say, I'm not giving up my strong coffee just yet,' Flint said, wiping the cream away from above his mouth. 'Anyway. Enough about my drinking habits. Tell me something. Relationships. I know you're single now. But before?'

The question initially took Dylan by surprise.

This surely wasn't anything to do with the case.

Maybe it was Flint wanting to get to know him better on a personal level. That was okay. In fact, Dylan liked it.

Maybe it was the sugar from the chocolate sprinkles inside him, but Dylan began to open up even more.

'I've had some nice relationships in the past,' Dylan said. 'Nothing that ever quite worked out. Most of them ran their natural course and then fizzled out. That happens.'

'Indeed it does,' Flint said, his soulful eyes meeting Dylan's gaze.

'But since starting cam work, it's been pretty much impossible,' Dylan continued. 'I'd like to meet someone. I mean, I'd really like to. But the camming lifestyle doesn't match up to having a secure, loving relationship. It definitely makes it a lot harder anyway. Too much drama.'

'I can see that,' Flint said, rubbing his hand over his beard. 'I'm guessing trust is a factor in that?'

Dylan nodded.

Trust was a *huge* factor.

Dylan's mind immediately though back to his last relationship.

His previous Daddy wanted nothing but sex. The fact they met through camming should have been a red flag. But Dylan had been taken in by his former Daddy's charms.

After a while, the warning signs had become rather more obvious. Dylan could see that his Daddy was essentially using him for sex.

It felt gross.

It felt worse than gross.

In fact, it was the worst thing he had experienced.

Dylan was sensitive.

He was deeply connected to his emotions.

Perhaps it explained his passion for acting and performance.

But when his Daddy was mean to him, or cold and distant, it really hit his confidence hard.

Of course, the final straw came when Dylan's former Daddy announced that he wanted to share Dylan with other Daddy Doms.

This felt like a betrayal.

It made Dylan feel worthless.

As Dylan explained this to Flint, he felt like a weight was being lifted. He had spoken about it with Casper, and one or two of his other Little friends.

But talking about it with a big, strong Daddy felt different.

Dylan could see that Flint was disgusted by the ex-Daddy.

'W-w-w-would you ever do something like that?' Dylan said, his voice trembling a touch.

'Never. Absolutely fucking not. No chance,' Flint said,

his voice suddenly booming again. 'Loyalty is everything to me. The way I see it, every important relationship has to have a deep sense of trust to it. That's the same whether I'm dealing with a victim on a case, or...'

Flint paused.

Dylan could tell that Flint wanted to say *between a Daddy and a Little* but had held himself back for some reason.

'I understand,' Dylan said, blushing a little. 'Well, how about you? Relationships I mean.'

Dylan felt his heart beat hard inside his chest.

He wasn't sure how Flint would react to being asked a question. So far, it had always been the other way round. Flint asking the questions and Dylan dutifully answering.

Flint got up from his seat and paced around the kitchen worktop. He picked up a whisky glass and inspected it. It was almost like he was stalling for time.

Then, putting the glass back down, Flint spoke.

'Well, first things first,' Flint said. 'You don't need to be nervous about asking me a question. Not now. Not ever. I want you to feel comfortable around me. Okay?'

Dylan nodded.

It felt good to know that Flint was thinking of his feelings.

Dylan also felt his dick stiffening up a little bit.

The way Flint spoke and carried himself was so masculine.

Dominant.

This was great.

However even the slightest exposure of his more caring, emotional side was like a shot of super-sugary juice.

'And to answer your question,' Flint said. 'No, I've never

60

been in a relationship. Not with a Little. But I am a Daddy. That's for sure.'

Dylan felt himself get hard again.

This time his dick really began to grow to full capacity.

It was like hearing Flint describing himself in no uncertain terms as being a Daddy was sexual rocket fuel.

Dylan tried to say something.

He wanted to reply.

But the words simply wouldn't come.

Maybe it was just as well because Flint wasn't done talking just yet.

'In my line of work, the risks are high,' Flint said, his mind somewhere else. 'The emotional toll can be a heavy one. I've learnt that the hard way. Trust me. Long hours too. I just figured that when it came to connecting with a Little, there would be too many complications. Too many risks. I'd never be able to live with myself if I hurt someone because of my actions. Or because of something related to my job.'

'I understand,' Dylan said. 'I can see how important your job is to you. It's like it's more than a job. It's your passion.'

'That's right,' Flint said, running his hands through his short hair. 'It can be tough. I've had to pay the ultimate price on occasion too. Still, enough of the negatives. We're here now. Right?'

Dylan smiled.

It was amazing to see Flint being so open.

Dylan knew that there would be drama from Flint's past.

That much was evident.

But there was a clear desire from Flint to change.

Even if he was only hinting at it.

Dylan felt like he could be a part of that change.

'What if there was a way of being in a relationship and staying true to your work?' Dylan said, hoping to keep Flint rolling. 'If I could help to be a part of that, it would be brilliant. I would make it fun too!'

Flint smiled.

Dylan was a naturally passionate and fun-loving person.

Ironically, it was one of the characteristics that his cam-customers seemed to love the most about him.

It was heart-warming for Dylan to see that his upbeat personality was having a positive effect on Flint.

He could tell that Flint didn't open up like this very often, if ever. So, for Dylan to be the one benefitting from it was something to cherish.

'I want to learn more. About whom I am. About how being in a Daddy and Little relationship could work,' Flint said, walking over to the large fruit bowl and taking out a huge, super-shiny red apple. 'Okay. Speaking of which. There's something I have to show you.'

'A surprise?' Dylan exclaimed, his eyes widening with excitement. 'I love surprises!'

'Okay, well just hold your horses, Mister,' Flint said, a tone of caution in his voice. 'Just wait until you know what it is first.'

But it was too late.

Dylan's mind was already working in overdrive trying to figure out what the surprise in store for him was.

He loved surprises.

Always had done.

And if Flint was potentially going to be his Daddy, what he had up his sleeve in this moment was of great interest to Dylan.

Immediately, Dylan was casting his eyes all over the

apartment, looking for clues as to what Flint's surprise could be.

He didn't spot any obvious clues.

But then again, Dylan didn't know what he was looking for either.

Flint stood with his arms folded across his chest.

A devilishly handsome grin broke out over his face.

Dylan had no idea what was coming his way.

The only question now was how he would react when the truth was revealed to him.

Chapter Eight

Flint rolled his eyes and smiled as he watched on. Dylan was obviously trying to work out what the surprise was.

It was so cute.

Flint almost felt tempted to leave Dylan hanging and not reveal the surprise. See how far he could push the cuteness overload.

There was something intoxicating about holding that power. In fact, it wasn't a million miles away from one of Flint's biggest kinks.

Flint enjoyed nothing more than orgasm control and denial.

But right in that moment, Flint knew that even he couldn't possibly keep Dylan waiting for a second longer.

'*Pleeeeease* tell me! Dylan said, almost squealing with delight. 'You can't say you've got a surprise and then hold out. That's a real stinky pants move!'

'*Hmm*, I wouldn't normally accept such sass, but I'll let it slide,' Flint said, tutting. 'Okay. You want the surprise?'

'Yes! Yes! Yes!'

'Well here it is,' Flint said, taking a piece of paper out from his kitchen drawer and placing it down on the table in front of Dylan. 'Surprise!'

Flint laughed at Dylan's shocked response.

It wasn't so much shock though.

More like a muted disbelief.

'My surprise is a boring piece of paper?' Dylan said. 'Is this a rental agreement or something?'

'Ha! Rental agreement?' Flint said, his voice echoing off the walls. 'Do I look like a realtor?'

Dylan shook his head.

'Well, have a read then,' Flint said. 'Then tell me if you think it's boring.'

Within seconds, the look on Dylan's face had totally changed.

This very much was not a boring rental agreement.

It was a BDSM contract.

'Would this mean I was your Little?' Dylan said, his voice a mixture of excited adrenalin and trepidation.

'We'll see,' Flint said. 'I think this is the only way to go if we want to explore our options. See what kind of future we could have together. Don't you?'

Dylan nodded before quickly burying his head in the contract again.

'So many options, so many... kinks,' Dylan stammered, clearly excited by what he was reading.

Damn, this is great.

I don't know who's more excited. Me or Dylan...

Flint strode over to the table and sat down next to Dylan.

The pair of them began to go through the contract together.

They talked about hard and soft limits.

What they would and wouldn't be prepared to do.

This was less stressful than Flint had imagined. Dylan was pretty comfortable talking about sexual matters. Probably because of his cam work.

Flint found himself able to be open and relaxed too.

There was something infectious about Dylan's enthusiasm.

It was rare that people had this type of effect on Flint. Ever since his police partner died, he had found relaxation incredibly difficult. Loosening up around other people just hadn't been on the agenda.

How could it have been?

If Flint wasn't able to relax in his own company, then it really was never going to be an option with other people.

But with Dylan it was different.

Very different.

'Okay, we need a safeword,' Flint said. 'I don't know what you think, but for me it's essential.'

'Definitely, and I've got the perfect word,' Dylan said, smiling. 'Juicebox.'

'Juicebox?' Flint said, raising an eyebrow. 'Okay, I'm sure you have your reasons. Juicebox it is.'

Dylan laughed and leant into Flint.

The feeling of Dylan nestling into his body made Flint's senses fire up. It was electric.

In that moment, Flint wanted nothing more than to devour every inch of Dylan.

Play with him.

Tease him.

Have his way with him.

But Flint knew he had to keep his cool.

They still needed to discuss things further.

'I think we should talk about, you know, *kinks*,' Flint said, taking the heat out of the situation by gently but firmly lifting Dylan into an upright sitting position. 'You go first.'

Dylan blushed a little.

Then he giggled.

'Don't make me spank it out of you,' Flint said, a playful but firm tone to his voice. 'Come on. Kinks. Talk.'

'I really like...'

'Spit it out! Remember, I could always get my paddle!'

'Well I love the thought of being tied up,' Dylan said, immediately bursting into a fit of giggles. 'Like, extreme bondage. Being tied up and left for a while. That kind of thing.'

'Interesting,' Flint said, purring with delight, his Daddy Dom senses almost spinning out of control. 'We can certainly work with that.'

'But it has to be safe,' Dylan added. 'I guess I've got trust issues. You know, after my last Daddy.'

'That's very understandable,' Flint said, knowing that helping Dylan to trust again was going to be his big challenge. 'Don't worry. I'm going to make it my mission to have you feeling as safe as possible.'

Dylan was practically glowing.

It felt good for Flint to see him have this kind of effect on someone.

Especially a Little like Dylan.

For so long, Flint had felt himself to be way too cynical and dysfunctional for a Little. Years of grinding out the casework and investigating some brutal crimes had worn away his ability to communicate and show his softer side.

Plus of course the tragedy with his ex-partner, Mickie.

But being with Dylan was different somehow.

'Your turn!' Dylan squealed, breaking Flint out of his daydream.

'My turn?'

'Yes, silly! Your turn to tell me *your* kinks!' Dylan laughed, playfully nudging his elbow into Flint's rock-solid stomach. 'I told you mine, now you tell me yours. That's how it works!'

Flint took a moment to compose himself.

It all sounded fine in his head but now the time had come for him to talk about his own kinks he felt himself clam up a little bit.

But he knew he had to talk.

That was part of the deal.

And Flint wasn't a man to back down from a deal.

It just wasn't his style.

Flint had too much honor for that.

'I'll count you in on three,' Dylan said, a slight hint of mischief in his voice. 'Three... two... one... go!'

'Okay, okay, I'll talk,' Flint said. 'I'm into orgasm control. Orgasm denial too. Basically, I get to control and be in charge of when my partner cums. So...'

Dylan was blushing.

Flint figured this was a positive sign.

It was certainly better than had Dylan stood up and run out of the apartment at a hundred miles per hour.

'I like the sound of it,' Dylan said, finally speaking. 'It could be really hot.'

'There's one catch to all this,' Flint said, his firm tone of voice back in full effect. 'No more camming. It's a deal breaker for me.'

'Oh,' Dylan replied, looking a little bit stunned at Flint's demand. 'I, um...'

Flint felt his heart sink.

It wasn't the response he had hoped for.

In truth, Flint had no idea how Dylan would respond. He hadn't really thought it through that much, it was just something that had come to him.

'It's okay, I understand,' Flint said. 'I can't share you with anyone. Not even via online activities. It's not compatible with who I am. If it's a problem for you, I get it. No worries. I would understand. Maybe we're just not meant to be.'

Flint's words trailed off.

He felt glum.

But at least he'd been honest and laid out exactly how he felt from the start.

This would minimize the damage in the longer run.

That was *something* at least.

Then, almost to Flint's total disbelief, Dylan leant over toward him again.

Except this time, he wasn't coming in for a snuggle.

Dylan moved in for a kiss.

The feeling of Dylan's soft, large lips on Flint's stubbly beard made Flint's pupils dilate. It was like all his senses were connected and feeling the kind of natural high that was very rare.

Certainly, in Flint's life up to that point it was a rarity.

Flint felt a desire to strip Dylan naked right that second and have his way with him. From the way that Dylan's hands were moving over Flint's lap, Flint felt sure that Dylan would be into it.

Probably in a major way.

But, again, Flint's sensible side just about regained control.

They hadn't signed the contract yet.

'I love the fact you want me to stop camming,' Dylan said. 'It's nice to be wanted so much. In such a wholesome, caring way too. Not everything is about sex. Even though that's a whole lot of naughty fun!'

'Indeed,' Flint said, his throbbing cock raging inside his pants.

'I'm glad you're willing to give camming up,' Flint said. 'It's no way for you to make a living. Especially as you don't enjoy it either. But speaking of money...'

'It's cool, I'll find another way to earn a living,' Dylan said, sounding full of optimism. 'It's a big city, and I'm sure I can turn my hand to anything if I really try. I might even find something that has a connection to the theatre. Try and get in at entry level.'

'That's my boy,' Flint said, proud to see Dylan taking the initiative and showing good resilience. 'Just because you're a Little, it doesn't mean you can't take control of situations that affect you.'

'Yes, Daddy,' Dylan said, taking on Flint's words. 'Giving up the camming is an easy decision to be honest. It's not only about the money though. I just want to be yours. That's if you'll have me?'

Flint felt a surge of pride.

This felt *right*.

It felt natural to him in a way that a relationship should.

In that moment, the pair of them went for the pen to sign the contract at the same time.

'You first, Daddy!' Dylan said.

'No, a true Daddy always thinks of his Little first,' Flint said. 'You go first. And that's an order!'

Dylan giggled, his cheeks burning red from excitement as he signed the contract.

Flint took the pen from Dylan's delicate hand and signed his space on the contract too.

It was official.

The real fun was about to begin.

Chapter Nine

The evening sky was turning dark.

This hopefully meant that a shower was on its way to break the suffocating heat.

If anything, the heatwave had been getting more intense.

Not that either Flint or Dylan cared at that moment.

Since signing the contract, the pair of them had felt incredibly happy and excited at what was to come.

Dylan had noticed the bulge in Flint's trousers, and it had only served to make him even harder too. He had so wanted for Flint to take control and let his hands run wild over his body.

But Dylan understood that they had to sign the contract.

After all, if Flint said that was the only option, then it probably was.

Even now so early in their relationship, Dylan felt comfortable that Flint knew what was best for him.

Dylan sensed it from the bottom of his heart that Flint had his best interests at heart.

It was a good feeling, something that Dylan had been searching for over a very long time indeed.

Before they left the apartment, Dylan had taken his cell phone out of his pocket and sent over a message to Casper, his Little BFF.

Wowie! I've got some seriously BIG news for you! Like, totally DADDY-RELATED news!!!! Will say more later. I'm going on a mystery date now. Can't wait to find out where! Dylan XoXo

Even as they had prepared to leave Flint's apartment, Dylan had felt the same surge or horniness towards Flint as he had earlier.

It was like Flint was his dream Daddy manifested into real life.

Of course, Dylan had been hurt before.

So even though he was super-excited, there was still a tiny little voice at the back of his mind. Talking. Causing mischief. Trying to instill a bit of doubt.

That doubting voice though was drowned out by Dylan's desire for Flint.

But before anything naughty could happen, it was time for a date.

But where were they heading?

'Come on, Flint, where are we going?' Dylan said.

He wasn't quite ready to call Flint *Daddy* in public, and it was evident from Flint's face that he was okay with that.

It appeared as if Flint instinctively understood that things might take time.

Dylan didn't think it would be long though.

Things were going so swimmingly well that it felt like only a matter of time before he was proudly proclaiming Flint to be his Daddy across the entire city.

'Please, *pretty please* tell me?' Dylan said, frustrated at Flint's decision to keep the surprise going.

'Enough!' Flint barked. 'You'll see when we get there.'

'Sorry, Daddy,' Dylan said, the sensation of being mildly disciplined turning him on something crazy. 'I'll be patient.'

'Good boy,' Flint said. 'A young man like you should be able to maintain their discipline better. Don't worry though, I'll help you learn. Sometimes the longer you have to wait, the better.'

Dylan couldn't help but smile.

He's talking about the orgasm control and denial.

Squee! I can't wait to experience some of that!

The pair continued to walk.

The New York streets were busy. It seemed like not even a stifling heatwave and possibly impending storm could keep people from having fun.

'Don't worry, we're close,' Flint said.

'*Hmmm*, I know these streets pretty well,' Dylan said, his mind beginning to join the dots. 'Are we going to... the theatre?'

Flint didn't respond.

But the grin on his face told its own story.

'Here we are,' Flint said, turning the corner and arriving at the entrance to the Golden House Theatre. 'Two tickets. Best seats in the house.'

Dylan was so excited.

This was a dream.

He had actually wanted to see the show, but the tickets were so expensive.

Way out of his budget.

For Flint to buy the tickets was one thing. It was super generous and kind. But for Flint to just know that this was a show that Dylan desperately wanted to see was another.

It was more than just good luck.

It was a deeper connection between them.

'Thank you so much, Daddy!' Dylan said, jumping up and down and hugging Flint. 'You know me so well! I've been wanting to see this for ages!'

'Hey, well let's hope it lives up to the hype,' Flint said, taking Dylan by the hand as they walked in through the golden double doors and into the large, ornately decorated foyer.

'Even if it stinks, it won't matter,' Dylan said. 'Being here with you is everything! It's all I need.'

With that, the pair walked through towards the main stage and took their seats.

* * *

The play was *superb*.

From the opening curtain to the final scene, it was an emotional journey full of laughter and joy.

It was exactly what both Dylan and Flint needed.

The pair of them had a brilliant time.

'Wow, that was one of the best nights I've had in such a long time,' Dylan said as they left the theatre. 'Did you enjoy it?'

Dylan looked at Flint.

He wasn't sure if Flint would have enjoyed the play as much as him. Dylan figured that Flint had bought the tickets mainly for him.

'I have to admit I loved it,' Flint said. 'It's not often I'm able to switch my mind off entirely. But I did. I wouldn't have gone if it wasn't for you, so I think really I'm the one who should be saying thank you.'

Dylan felt all warm inside.

To know that he was positively impacting Flint's life was a nice feeling. He only hoped it could continue.

As they walked away from the theatre, Dylan suddenly felt his energy levels dip.

It was like he was crashing from the high of the theatre experience.

But there was more to it.

'Everything okay?' Flint said, putting his hand on Dylan's shoulder. 'You seem a little bit deflated?'

Flint paused.

Dylan stopped walking and looked at Flint.

The storm still hadn't broken, and the heat was stifling.

Wiping away the sweat from his forehead, Dylan spoke.

'The thing is, I've always dreamed of being on Broadway myself,' Dylan said. 'Being here and seeing this play was incredible. I loved it more than a million marsh-mallows. But the thing is...'

Dylan was struggling to finish his sentence.

He could feel his bottom lip trembling a little bit.

This was embarrassing.

'Hey, come on, it's okay,' Flint said. 'I get it. You wanted to be up on that stage. That makes sense. Instead of being upset, why not use it as motivation?'

'Huh?'

'I mean, take this experience for what it is,' Flint said. 'You were checking out the talent out there. Seeing how you compare. I've never seen you act but I know for sure that you've got it in you. If Broadway is what you want, you'll make it. And I'll be there every step of the way with you. Right?'

I'm so lucky.

Flint always knows what to say...

'You're right,' Dylan said, a hint of resolve in his voice. 'I *will* use it as motivation!'

Dylan felt so much better.

And all it took was a twenty second pep-talk from Flint.

Holding hands, the pair of them took a short walk down the block and sought refuge in a bar that Dylan knew had super-good aircon.

Flint drank a cold beer while Dylan opted for a crushed-ice apple and mango juice.

'OMG, this is too good,' Dylan squealed.

He had practically downed the entire drink in less than ten seconds.

'*Hmmm*, I'll get you another,' Flint said. 'But next time, make it last. Got it?'

'Yes, Sir!' Dylan said, a little giddy from the cold juice.

As Flint waited to be served at the busy bar, Dylan took his cell phone out to have a quick look.

There was a message from Casper.

Tell me everything!!! I neeeeeed to know the deets!!!! This sounds tooooo exciting!!!! Gotta go, working on finishing the latest webcomic by tonight's deadline. Casper XoXo

Dylan loved to see how well Casper's webcomic was doing. It brought a lot of pride and self-worth for Casper. Dylan wished he could feel the same about his work.

Maybe with Flint's support he would be able to achieve his Broadway dreams.

It may have been the sugary juice talking, but in that moment *anything* seemed possible.

Dylan watched as Flint spoke with the barman.

There was something so assured about how Flint carried himself.

He was confident, but not arrogant.

In control, but not rude or obnoxious.

People respected him.

Dylan couldn't quite believe that they were a couple. It was almost too good to be true. Briefly, Dylan's mind flashed back to his former Daddy.

That was never good.

The pain that Dylan had experienced in that so-called relationship was something he never, *ever* wanted to feel again.

His ex-Daddy could be so callous.

Cruel even.

He barely respected Dylan on even the most basic levels. The idea that he would have thought to do a BDSM contract like Flint had would never have occurred to him.

That's the past.

It's over now.

Now I've got Flint...

As Flint returned with the fresh drink, plus a new beer for himself, the pair began to talk.

'Okay, so here's a curveball,' Flint said. 'I actually love romance novels. Don't laugh! I know it's a bit odd.'

Dylan smiled.

It wasn't odd at all.

Maybe a little unexpected, but not odd.

'No way! I do too!' Dylan said, beaming with joy. 'I'll get through two or three a week. Sometimes more!'

'You don't think it's strange that a New York City cop is into romance novels?' Flint said, his eyebrow raised. 'You can admit it if you do.'

Dylan shook his head.

'Well, maybe it's not top of the list of things I would have guessed about you,' Dylan conceded. 'But it's totally brilliant. We've got things in common. I love it!'

'I guess cozy nights in front of the fire reading are on our to-do list then,' Flint said, his Adam's apple flexing as he gulped down his beer.

Dylan loved the sound of the nighttime reading, but there was something on his mind.

'There's one thing, it's about me being a Little,' Dylan said. 'I'm a bit scared that I'll embarrass myself when I'm in Little Space.'

Flint raised his eyebrow.

Dylan decided to keep talking.

'It's maybe the biggest fear that Littles have with new partners,' Dylan continued. 'Like, if I'm really into coloring or having a stuffie cuddle, I might come over as too much for you? Too Little?'

Flint shook his head.

'No, don't worry about me,' Flint said. 'You can be exactly whoever you want to be. I have a feeling I'm going to like it. No, actually I have a feeling I'm going to *love* it.'

This was so reassuring to hear.

What was even more reassuring was the way that Flint took Dylan's hand and cupped it between his two large hands.

The pair of them shared a moment of eye contact.

Flint's piercing gray-blue eyes and Dylan's soft hazel eyes.

The heat between them was rising.

Maybe it was time to leave...

* * *

Back at Flint's place, it was bedtime.

Dylan felt his heart pound as Flint led him into his bedroom.

The big bed was freshly made, the sheets perfectly straight and looking inviting.

It was late, and definitely past Dylan's bedtime.

Dylan felt a little bit self-conscious getting changed before bed.

Flint's body looked absolutely incredible. He had the kind of natural fitness and muscle tone that only the lucky few were blessed with.

'This is what you get after years of working the city streets,' Flint joked, his stomach muscles tightening as he laughed. 'Now, given the heat I suggest you just wear pajama bottoms. No top.'

Dylan agreed.

It felt thrilling to be taking instructions from Flint.

Dylan's submissive side was coming to the fore. It felt good.

It also made him feel like he wanted to be naughty.

'Okay, bed. And you can forget about any sexy ideas you might have,' Flint said sternly. 'It's late and you need to get some shut-eye.'

'*Awwww!*' Dylan pleaded, snuggling next to Flint and running his hand over Flint's impressive abs.

'No means no, kid,' Flint said, a little sternly. 'However... we can have a story.'

With the aircon in the room providing respite from the suffocating heat, Flint tucked Dylan into bed and they began to co-read a bedtime story.

Dylan provided the character voices and relished it.

It was almost like acting practice.

But the pressure was off.

He wasn't being judged.

It was all about the fun.

'Hey, you're pretty damn good at this,' Flint said. 'It gives me an idea.'

'Yes, Daddy?' Dylan replied, interested in what Flint could be hinting at.

'No. I'll tell you in the morning.'

'Daddy! *Awww*, okay then,' Dylan said, knowing full well that once Flint said something, he meant it.

Dylan knew he would have to wait.

But that was okay.

As Dylan drifted off to sleep, he was happy to have had such an enjoyable evening with Flint.

The only question was what surprises would the coming days bring?

Chapter Ten

The night shift had been tough.

There had been plenty going on, as always.

Even the mid-shift tradition of one of the junior cops heading out to buy some sweet and savory snacks wasn't as satisfyingly delicious as normal.

Put simply, it was just too hot to eat.

Although plenty of new cases were coming in, Flint still very much had his eye on Dylan's case.

So far, no joy.

With the total lack of evidence available, it was hard to see how the hell they could make any kind of tangible breakthrough.

This was frustrating for Flint.

Extremely frustrating in fact.

There was nothing that bothered him more than a case that simply had no leads attached to it. If Flint had something – anything at all – he could work with, that would be a start.

But so far, nothing.

Nothing at all.

Flint had even returned to Dylan's apartment building to try and see if there were any other cleaners or even residents he could speak with.

Another total strike-out.

Somewhere, the perpetrator of the crime was still out there.

The thought of this crime going unpunished hurt Flint.

Someone as kindhearted and innocent as Dylan didn't deserve this to happen to them. No one did, in truth. But given Flint's relationship with Dylan, it was perhaps understandable that it irked him even more.

As the shift carried on, it was a case of alternating cold glasses of water with coffee.

Despite the oppressive heat, Flint had downed coffee after coffee, the caffeine eventually wearing off as his shift drew to a close.

'Okay, I'm out,' Flint said, waving to the detective replacing him. 'Have a good one.'

'You too, Flint,' the new detective replied, already weary looking and only seconds into his shift.

Police work could be hard going.

But if Flint really was a Hero Daddy, then he just had to get on with it. Which he did, with no real complaint.

Police work was his passion.

But that wasn't to say that he couldn't also feel a sense of relief when a particularly tough day was over.

As Flint walked home, he felt something that he hadn't experienced in a very long time.

He actually *wanted* to get home.

There was a reason for him to leave work.

A motivating factor in his life other than solving criminal cases and putting bad guys away behind bars.

Of course, that reason was Dylan.

That being said, Flint had still been spending a lot of time in the office. The extra-hot weather had seen a rise in crime.

It always did.

But this time it was like people were acting totally crazy.

A less experienced detective would potentially have struggled with the intensity of the increased work.

But Flint took it all in his stride.

And kept on working at his own thorough pace too.

But it wasn't just Flint who was getting super-involved with work.

Dylan had been pursuing a new dream too.

After being so impressed with Dylan's character voices during their bedtime story, Flint had set up a recording studio for him in his apartment.

It was great to see Dylan committing to something that he was passionate about. And Dylan was seriously talented at it as well.

When Flint arrived home, he was extra careful to not make any noise.

As he suspected, Dylan was in the middle of a recording session. Flint chuckled very quietly to himself as he heard Dylan switching from one cutesy voice to another.

It was impressive to listen to.

Dylan was using his own laptop as the recorder, but Flint had bought Dylan a professional quality microphone and some equally impressive home studio software.

Flint knew that Dylan was passionate about performance, so the cost was irrelevant. He wanted to do whatever it took to make Dylan feel that he had a shot at succeeding in showbiz.

It may not be Broadway yet, but it was a start.

That was for sure.

Flint carefully walked into the kitchen area of the apartment and took out a cold beer from the refrigerator. He expertly opened the bottle with minimum fuss, the tiniest of fizzing noises coming out of the bottle.

Satisfied that he wasn't disturbing Dylan, Flint took a slug of the beer.

It tasted *good*.

It was just what Flint needed after an exhausting and at times stressful shift. Plenty of work and not enough time to do it. It was always the way.

Suddenly, the sound of Dylan's voice stopped.

'Hey! You're home. Why didn't you come and say hello?' Dylan said, popping his head out of the guest bedroom door.

'Didn't want to disturb you,' Flint said, his tiredness vanishing as he saw Dylan's exuberance. 'Good session?'

Dylan smiled shyly.

'It sure was,' Dylan said.

There was something he wasn't saying.

Flint could always tell when information was being withheld.

Call it one of the perks of being a highly seasoned detective.

But what was Dylan holding back?

'Are you going to say any more or do I have to find out another way?' Flint said. 'Remember, not only am I an expert in interrogation, I'm also a Daddy Dom.'

'*Hehe*,' Dylan sniggered. 'Okay, okay. I was recording a sexy little play today. Things definitely were getting a bit on the steamy side. Well, more than a bit steamy in fact.'

Flint was interested in this.

Not only was he impressed with Dylan's confidence,

but he was also extremely turned on by the thought of Dylan letting his imagination run wild as he recorded.

Flint had to hear the recording.

'I think it's time you played me this recording,' Flint said, firmly but with a smile creeping over his face. 'That's not a request, by the way.'

Flint could see Dylan respond to his authoritative tone.

'Come with me then,' Dylan said, eager and ready to please his Daddy. 'I don't usually enjoy listening back to myself, but this time could be a bit different.'

The pair of them went into the guestroom, now home recording studio.

Flint had purchased some soundproofing foam strips to go over the windows. The effect of this was that the room was darker than it might otherwise have been.

This only added to the mood.

'I'll take a seat here, I think,' Flint said, lowering his frame into the comfortable armchair next to the bed. 'When you're ready. I'm all ears.'

Flint watched as Dylan nervously fiddled around with his MacBook Air. It was quite clear that Dylan was a little jumpy, possibly worried that Flint wouldn't like the recording.

Flint wanted to put Dylan at ease.

He knew the recording would be superb, but it was important that Dylan had this level of self-belief in himself to go along with his natural talent.

'Take a breath, I know this is going to rock,' Flint said, taking a slow gulp from his beer bottle. 'Remember, I wouldn't have helped get you this equipment if I didn't think you were the cat's pajamas. Would I?'

Dylan nodded sweetly.

Flint liked the feeling of being a reassuring presence in

Dylan's life. He had to momentarily stop himself from getting angry at the thought of Dylan's former Daddy not treating him with the respect he so clearly deserved.

That was then, focus on Dylan's future with you...

'Okay, ready?' Flint said, adjusting his seating position for maximum comfort. 'I can't wait to get into this.'

'Well just to warn you, it does get pretty frisky,' Dylan giggled.

Dylan pressed play and then immediately jumped up onto the bed and buried himself under a pile of pillows.

'No need to be shy,' Flint said. 'I'm sure it's nothing I haven't heard before.'

The pair of them laughed as the recording began.

Within a couple of minutes, it was clear the direction that the play was taking. In his recording, Dylan had set up a situation where an angry, grumpy mountain man catches a young villager trespassing on his property.

What followed was scene after scene of the mountain man stripping, punishing and playing with the villager.

Teasing and tormenting him.

Bending him over, exposing him.

Giving him equal measures of pleasure and pain.

To say it was a little bit on the adult side was an understatement...

'This is out and out X-Rated stuff!' Flint said, whooping with joy as the recording played out a scene where the mountain man inserted a hand-crafted butt-plug inside the innocent villager. 'I should take notes. Something tells me that this is the kind of thing you might enjoy happening in real life!'

Dylan giggled and buried his head deep into the plump white pillow.

As the recording continued, Flint couldn't help but be impressed by Dylan's professionalism and craft.

But honestly, what was really captivating Flint was just how dirty the story was.

The steam-factor was practically in orbit it was so high.

Flint's body was reacting too.

He couldn't remember the last time he was so hard.

The feeling of his dick straining to escape his pants was relentless. It was like he had a never-ending boner. The only way things could change would be...

'Come over here,' Flint said, the recording drawing to a close. 'Sit on my lap. Now.'

Dylan immediately jumped off the bed and made his way over to Flint. He could tell that Flint wasn't joking around.

It was time to obey.

Flint witnessed Dylan gasp as he felt Flint's rock-hard dick press up against his tight sweatpants.

'You've only got yourself to blame for getting me so riled up,' Flint said. 'That was seriously hot. Tell me though. Did you have anyone in mind when it came to the mountain man?'

Dylan giggled.

'Well, you could say I had some inspiration close to home,' Dylan said, a wicked smile on his face. 'I always like to channel what's going on in my personal life. That's where the real juice comes from.'

Flint nodded.

It was impressive to hear Dylan taking his art so seriously.

But further artistic exploration could wait.

Flint had something else he wanted to explore.

And that was Dylan.

Flint cupped Dylan's sweet face in his hands and as their lips touched, the electricity between them went wild.

Before they knew it, their hands were all over each other.

Flint loved the feeling of Dylan's smaller, far more slender body.

It was perfection as far as Flint could tell.

There was something incredibly sexy too about the way Dylan was allowing Flint to manhandle him.

Firmly.

Totally in control.

Dylan was enjoying every second of his submission.

That was until Flint noticed something.

Both of them were topless at this point, the contrast between their two torsos making a perfect combination of Daddy and Little sexiness.

But when Flint looked down and saw Dylan rubbing his own cock, something had to give.

'You do *not* touch yourself without my permission!' Flint bellowed. 'I am absolutely in control of that body. I'm in charge of your pleasure. It looks like I might have to teach you a lesson!'

Dylan gasped as Flint stood up from the chair with Dylan in his arms.

Flint's strength was incredible.

As was his desire to show his Little exactly who was in charge.

Dylan would have to get used to working with a director rather than running his own show.

From this point onwards, it would be Flint calling the shots.

Chapter Eleven

He's so powerful!
Dominant!
I love it...

Dylan was barely able to process what was going on. He was so turned on. It was like his entire brain had melted into one big slushy pile of horniness.

And it was all down to Flint.

Even as he had been recording the play in his home studio, Dylan found his mind wandering to Flint over and over again.

Images of Flint naked.

Aroused.

Prowling up and down, with a look of hunger on his face.

In truth, the character of the mountain man wasn't so much inspired by Flint as a direct cut and paste of him!

And now Dylan found himself slowly but surely being tied up by Flint. It was like his body was perfectly malleable, ready and waiting for Flint to do with it exactly as he wished.

Flint didn't need any encouragement either.

Like a true Daddy, he was more than comfortable in taking total control of the situation.

Of course, the pair of them had their safeword ready just in case.

On top of that, both had agreed that this was a monogamous relationship and as they were both tested and clear, there would be no need for protection either.

'Do you like it?' Flint said, the gruffness in his voice making Dylan quiver with arousal. 'The feeling of being tied up... helpless... vulnerable to whatever I want to do to you?'

Dylan could almost have orgasmed just from listening to Flint.

In fact, the thought crossed Dylan's mind that Flint could act in one of his future recordings.

But that was an idea very much for another time.

Right in that moment it was all about the here and now.

'It's tight... I like it,' Dylan said, aware that he was already breathing heavily from excitement. 'My whole body likes it actually.'

Dylan looked down and saw that his exposed dick was standing to attention.

'So I see,' Flint said, walking around Dylan, lightly tracing his heavy fingers over his body. 'But remember, it's me who says when you get your release. That's if I let you have it at all.'

'Yes, sir,' Dylan said. 'I understand exactly. I want you to do to me exactly what you want.'

'Good. That's what I like to hear,' Flint replied sternly. 'I think we'll begin with some punishment.'

'Punishment?' Dylan gasped. 'B-b-b-but...'

'No buts,' Flint said. 'You were very bad. You touched

your cock without my permission. You know that's not allowed. Not on my watch. As such, there will have to be a price to be paid.'

Dylan's head was spinning with excitement.

Even the lightest touch from Flint was making him tremble.

How he'd react with whatever punishment was coming his way was anyone's guess.

'Now, let's see if we can get this sassy little peach of an ass nice and red,' Flint laughed, taking a big swipe with his hand and expertly landing it down on Dylan's left butt cheek. 'One!'

Flint proceeded to alternate the spanks between each cheek.

Each spank was hard.

Accurate.

A sign to Dylan that Flint knew exactly what he was doing.

Dylan was in safe hands.

Safe, but capable of inflicting deliciously stingy spanks.

'*Awwww!*' Dylan yelped as yet another loud crack of Flint's hand landed on his ass. 'I deserve it! But it hurts!'

'You do deserve it, and you're lucky I'm not using a paddle this time!' Flint bellowed, launching into one final flurry of spanks that had Dylan yelping. 'I think that's enough for now. Got anything to say for yourself, young man?'

Dylan paused to get his breath back.

Being spanked was hard work.

'Yes, I want to thank you for the spanking,' Dylan said. 'I needed it. And I promise to be better from now on.'

Dylan enjoyed the feeling of being so submissive.

Not even trying to dispute Flint's punishment.

Dylan knew that he'd had it coming. It was in the BDSM contract they'd signed.

Flint was in control of all things when it came to pleasure.

That was just the way it was now.

And Dylan was more than happy with things that way.

'Now I think it's time to repay you for taking your punishment so well,' Flint said, his voice almost purring with delight.

Dylan felt Flint adjust his body position somewhat so that Dylan's legs were parted slightly further apart.

He was still tied tightly and securely though.

There was absolutely no escaping whatever it was that Flint had planned for him.

'W-w-w-w-what's going on back there?' Dylan said, spluttering over his words as he heard the low hum of vibrations.

'Take a guess,' Flint laughed.

Dylan let out a gasp of pleasure as he felt Flint part his ass cheeks and squirt a big dollop of lube over his perfectly pink ass hole.

'Oh my G–'

'Ha! You like that?' Flint said. 'Well let's see how much you enjoy this.'

Flint proceeded to pick up a small black buttplug and tease it around Dylan's hole. There was sheer joy in Flint's voice as he commanded Dylan to relax and take the plug inside him.

'Don't worry, there's way more where this came from,' Flint chuckled as he finally eased the plug all the way in. 'Bigger too. Much, *much* bigger!

Flint wasn't kidding.

Dylan proceeded to take plug after plug inside hit tight butt.

Each one larger than the last.

Finally, it was time for him to take the biggest.

It was also the one with the vibrator built into it.

'Ready?' Flint said, gripping Dylan's thighs and reaching around to his dick. 'Remember, no cumming unless I say!'

'Y-y-y-yes,' Dylan stammered, knowing full well that it would be incredibly difficult to control himself for long. 'I'll do my bestest.'

'You'd better,' Flint warned, turning the vibrations up on the plug and delighting in the sight of Dylan's entire body tensing and releasing as the waves of vibrations coursed over him. 'This is so hot I might even cum right here and now. But not you. Don't forget that.'

Dylan was struggling.

He was so close to release.

But each time it looked like he was about to blow his top, Flint would find a way to bring him back off the ledge.

The first time, Flint simply stopped the vibrations dead in their tracks. The shock was enough to stop Dylan.

The second time, Flint was jerking Dylan off hard and fast with the aid of some lube.

Dylan was groaning.

His body *so close* to ecstasy.

Then, suddenly, Flint let go of his dick.

No more contact.

Dylan came off the ledge once more.

He didn't know how long he could cope with this.

But Flint wasn't done yet.

Dylan moaned as Flint began to jerk him off again. This time, he was going even faster. Finding the perfect rhythm instantly. Dylan was desperate to cum. He wanted it more than anything.

So much so that he decided to try and have his release.

Even though he knew it was going against what Flint wanted.

'Not so fast!' Flint laughed, noticing Dylan's thrusts. 'Busted!'

Flint wasn't about to let Dylan off the hook and immediately stopped working his dick. Instead, he focused his attention onto Dylan's nipples and gave them a firm, long squeeze.

'*Awwww!*' Dylan hollered, the exquisite pain of his nipples being pulled on by Flint nonetheless stopping his orgasm in its tracks.

For now, at least.

'You were very naughty to try and cum, weren't you?' Flint barked.

He sounded a little bit scary.

It was intense.

But the kind of intensity that Dylan could get on board with one hundred and ten percent.

'Yes, I did,' Dylan said. 'I'm sorry. You can punish me more if you want. I would deserve it. I'll do better next time.'

Flint was silent.

Dylan's mind was running wild with the possibilities of what Flint might do.

Was he going to get his paddle out?

Or maybe give Dylan another forty spanks with his bare hands?

Either option was going to be painful, that was for sure.

Or maybe Flint had a whole other plan in store to give Dylan the punishment he deserved.

The funny thing was, Dylan wasn't nervous at all.

He felt so safe.

Safe with Flint.

Safe also in the knowledge that whatever Flint did, it would be with the best intentions.

So it was something of a surprise then when instead of a punishment, Dylan felt Flint wrap his fist around his dick again.

This time, Flint started slowly.

He squeezed and made a pulsing motion with his balled-up fist.

Very quickly, Dylan's dick was rock-hard again.

'You're enjoying it,' Flint said, using his other hand to pull down on Dylan's balls.

'B-b-b-but I think I might cum?' Dylan gasped.

'That's the whole point,' Flint laughed. 'Go for it. Don't wait for me to change my mind, young man!'

Dylan didn't need telling twice.

After three orgasm denials, this was his chance to get a much-needed release. Before long, he could feel the semen build up and his balls tighten.

When Dylan came it was explosive.

Probably one of the best orgasms he had ever experienced.

He felt totally unselfconscious and let out an animalistic, high-pitched groan as he shot his load all over the floor beneath him.

It felt *incredible*.

Dylan could barely catch his breath.

'Have I been doing it wrong all these years?' Dylan final managed to say, his voice still wobbly and lacking any kind of usual rhythm.

'You just haven't had me in charge,' Flint said, a satisfied grin on his face as he towered over Dylan. 'I should add, I've never enjoyed doing that as much as I just did with you. Not close. Not even *remotely close* in fact.'

This felt lovely to hear.

Dylan felt a sense of pride that he had managed to last so long. Evidently, he had pleased Flint too.

This was a very special added bonus.

It also suggested that they had a strong sexual connection. It was all very well wanting a relationship, but you never really knew for sure until you got down to the physical side.

The way this had gone, Dylan felt sure that him and Flint would never have any issues in the bedroom.

And there was so much more left to explore too.

* * *

After some very tender aftercare, and a ton of soothing lotion on his red butt, Dylan was absolutely wiped out.

It was time for bed.

'Was everything okay earlier? Nothing you didn't like?' Flint said, genuinely wanting to know.

'No, it was perfect,' Dylan said. 'I loved every second of it. Maybe next time I can have even more denials. They felt so naughty.'

Flint laughed.

'I really didn't think you'd make it past the first one to be honest,' Flint said, tucking Dylan in. 'Maybe you're a natural at this? Who knows, I might be able to keep you teetering on the edge all day soon enough? Imagine that.'

Dylan blushed and giggled.

'Maybe I'll dream about that tonight!' Dylan squealed.

'*Hmm*, okay. But try not to get too worked up now, you

need a good night's sleep,' Flint said. 'I want to see you living your best Little life possible. And a big part of that is making sure that you get all of the sleep you need. How else are you going to carry on your impressive recording career?'

Dylan felt like he was falling for Flint.

Falling *hard*.

There was something so genuinely caring about him.

Dylan was lucky to have good Little friends. They would do anything for each other. But there was something extra special about having a Daddy who always had his back.

Flint definitely fell into that category.

'I wish you didn't have to go into work tomorrow, Daddy,' Dylan said, his eyes half-closing.

Dylan was close to falling asleep.

Before he knew it, Dylan was drifting off to snooze-town.

Dylan didn't even stay awake long enough to hear Flint's response to his question.

As it turned out, Dylan would have to wait until the morning to find out exactly what Flint had planned.

But until then, it was a case of counting sheep and getting his eight hours of sleep in.

Tomorrow would be another day.

One filled with *plenty* more fun and naughtiness on the agenda.

Chapter Twelve

BLEEP-BLEEP-BLEEP!

'Urgh, turn off!' Flint called out, irritated that his alarm was going off and more so that it wasn't responding to the voice command. 'I said: turn the hell off!'

Dylan giggled, much to Flint's annoyance.

'Hey, are you being a Grumpy Bear?' Dylan said, noticing the exasperated look on Flint's face as the alarm continued to bleep. 'I thought you'd be happy after all of our fun last night?'

Dylan had a point, and Flint knew it.

They had a great time the previous night, and Flint wanted more.

Probably the main source of his frustration wasn't the fact that the alarm was going.

He was totally used to early mornings.

No, it was something else.

It was the fact that he desperately didn't want to leave Dylan.

Not for the whole day.

Not even for a single minute if truth be told.

'I think you might have to get out of bed to turn it off!' Dylan said, bursting into laughter as Flint roughly tossed the cover off and hauled himself up and out of bed.

Flint had fallen asleep naked and woken up with something of a hard-on. As Flint turned from switching the alarm off, he noticed Dylan's eyes immediately casting down to his semi-hard length of meat.

'Like what you see, eh?' Flint said, a glint in his eye. 'Well, don't worry, I'm sure you'll be seeing a lot more of it soon enough.'

'*Hehe*, I hope so, Daddy!' Dylan squealed in joy, his cheeks red with embarrassment.

Dylan was evidently not used to seeing his Daddy in the nude yet.

'Come back to bed? Please?' Dylan said, hopefully.

'No, I'm up now,' Flint said sternly. 'Number one in my book of good habits is waking up when your alarm goes off. It sets the tone. Discipline is important, remember.'

Dylan scrunched his face up.

It looked a bit like a bratty show of defiance.

Flint wasn't in the mood to let it slide.

'I said, *up!*' Flint bellowed. 'Unless you fancy a brisk morning spanking? I could always use my paddle to warm you up?'

Flint's words did the trick.

In double-time too.

Before Flint could even say another word, Dylan had sprung up from the bed and was prancing out of the bedroom in his warm pajama top and bottoms.

Damn, he's got a cute tushy.

Flint momentarily caught himself staring as Dylan stopped to stretch his hands up into the air.

As he did, he clenched and released his butt.

It looked highly appetizing to Flint.

But that could wait.

It was breakfast time.

'Okay, I think we'll have a big bowl of muesli and a glass of my patented multi-berry smoothie to go with it,' Flint said.

'That sounds delicious,' Dylan said, climbing up onto the barstool in the kitchen. 'It looks like another hot day outside. Too hot to play in the park even.'

Dylan looked a little bit downhearted.

Flint didn't know everything about Dylan yet, but he knew how much he enjoyed playdates in the park. But if it was too hot to go outside, it didn't mean that Dylan couldn't have fun.

Far from it.

But Flint's plan could wait until after breakfast.

As the pair sat down to eat, a puzzled look came over Dylan's face.

'Daddy, aren't you leaving it a bit fine to make it into work?' Dylan said.

Flint didn't say anything.

Instead, he picked his cellphone up and held it to his ear.

Flint made a shushing noise as Dylan was about to speak.

'Yep, it's Detective Maddox,' Flint said, his voice sounding croaky and subdued. 'Yep. Yep. Trust me, I feel even worse than I sound. Probably a bug. Yep. Will keep you informed. Thank you, Sir.'

Flint looked across and saw a huge grin on Dylan's face.

'Daddy, are you playing hooky? That's naughty!' Dylan said, excitement all over his voice as he proceeded to take a big sip of his smoothie. 'You'd spank me if I ever did anything like that!'

Flint laughed.

Dylan was right.

Flint would definitely spank Dylan's butt if the situation was reversed.

'That's just one of the perks of being a Daddy,' Flint laughed. 'Anyway, aren't you pleased? We get to spend an extra day together.'

'I'm happier than the happiest unicorn in magical rainbow-land!' Dylan declared.

Dylan finished off his muesli and smoothie and Flint gave him permission to get down from the table and play.

Flint had ordered some crayons, paper, and coloring books from Amazon and before Dylan knew it, he was in a world of his own.

It felt magical for Flint to see Dylan so happy.

Magical almost.

Flint's blood ran cold when he considered the risk Dylan had been under when he was alone at his place.

But that feeling passed. Things were different now.

Dylan was safe.

Flint decided to let Dylan get on with his coloring. He had some emails to sort through.

Plus, it was time for him to renew his home insurance.

All boring adult tasks.

But with Dylan being so deep into his own fun, it felt like a good time to get on with it.

Once he was done with his mundane tasks, Flint looked down and saw that Dylan was still having fun and enjoying himself greatly.

Dylan seemed almost serene.

Like he was there, but his mind had been transported somewhere else a little bit at the same time.

'Are you... in Little Space?' Flint said. 'I must admit it's not something I'm an expert in. But you look so happy and relaxed. Natural too. It's a joy to see.'

Dylan turned and smiled.

Then he nodded.

Flint didn't need to hear Dylan confirm it in words, the answer to his question was obvious.

'Daddy, do you want to play a game?' Dylan said a few minutes later as he hung up a drawing of a rainbow with two unicorns walking up to the top of it. 'I think I've got one you might quite enjoy!'

Flint put down his iPad and arched his eyebrow.

'Sounds interesting,' Flint said. 'Tell me more.'

'Well, you know those stuffies you bought?' Dylan said, his voice full of hope and high spirits. 'How about we play a game of cops and robbers with them? Even better, we could put on a show!'

This wasn't exactly in Flint's wheelhouse of skills.

But as it was Dylan asking him, he wasn't about to put a dampener on things.

'Okay, but you know I'm not as good at voices as you, right?' Flint said. 'I'm no Robert DeNiro.'

Dylan laughed.

'Ha ha! That doesn't matter, you'll be brilliant! I know you will!' Dylan said, rushing over to the large wooden box with the stuffies spilling out over the top of.

Flint momentarily felt a little self-conscious.

His life was built around cracking cases and hunting down bad guys. The concept of putting on a play with a cast of stuffies wasn't exactly something he had done before.

Hell, it was something he'd never even *considered* up until this moment.

But he wasn't about to let Dylan down.

Dylan's fun was the most important thing to Flint.

He was determined to give the stuffie play his best shot.

'So, we're just making it up as we go along?' Flint said, taking a larger bear stuffie from Dylan. 'There's no pre-agreed process?'

Dylan rolled his eyes.

It was a bit bratty, but Flint found him so adorable he let it slide.

'Yes, Daddy, it's called improvisation,' Dylan said, almost asking to be flipped over onto Flint's lap and given a spanking. 'Everyone knows you improvise first before you put the proper script in place. Silly!'

Flint grumbled.

In fact, he felt like doing a lot more.

But before long, Flint actually surprised himself.

Not only was he enjoying himself...

But he was pretty good at this whole improvisation thing.

Well, *he* thought he was.

Dylan would be the real judge of that.

'Daddy, you're good at this!' Dylan declared, a bunny in one hand and a duckling in the other. 'Your big bad bear character is really great. But now it's time for Officer Flop and Detective Duck to catch him and lock his butt up!'

Flint couldn't help but laugh.

It was very sweet to see Dylan putting everything into this.

How could anyone ever want to make Dylan feel bad?

It just didn't make sense to Flint at all.

They continued to act out the play, eventually moving

on from the improvisations and putting together a simple three act structure.

It was a lot of fun.

Even a work-focused grouch like Flint had to admit that.

In between scenes, Flint got up from the floor and went to make himself a coffee and prepare a fresh juice for Dylan.

It was shaping up to be the perfect morning.

'*Aww*, I want coffee too!' Dylan said as Flint returned to the home-made theater set. 'No fair!'

Flint took a sip of his double espresso.

'Coffee is really for big guys like me,' Flint said. 'You can have some sometimes. But not today. What you need at the moment is lots of fresh fruit and vegetable juices. And that's exactly what you'll get. No complaints, Mister. Got it?'

Dylan nodded and took a big gulp of his juice.

'Well, it is tasty I guess,' Dylan said a little sulkily. 'Thank you for looking out for me so well, Daddy.'

Flint felt himself beam with pride.

It was a good moment.

Knowing just how much of a positive impact he was having on Dylan. The next step was to put together a career plan. Make sure that Dylan had the best possible chance to make the most of his undeniable talents.

But that could wait.

This morning was about fun.

And maybe a little bit of discipline too.

After finally completing the stuffie play, Dylan decided to do an encore. This involved sitting up on Flint's lap and the two main characters singing a little song to say goodbye to the audience.

It was extremely sweet.

But it was also exciting too...

'What on earth is that I see?' Flint said, a quietly stern tone to his voice. 'Right there, at the front of your pants?'

Dylan blushed.

He blushed hard.

With Dylan's cheeks bright red, he started to giggle.

'Come on, answer me. Right this second,' Flint said, the Daddy Dom side of his personality coming to front and center.

'It's just... sitting on your lap,' Dylan said. 'I can feel... your... big *thing* underneath my tush.'

Flint wanted to ravage Dylan right there and then.

But he maintained control over his desires.

This was not the time.

'*Hmm*, I did not give permission,' Flint said.

Flint quickly flipped Dylan over and gave a rapid-fire ten spanks on his ass.

'Bad boy,' Flint said, firmly holding Dylan in position. 'You're lucky these are over your pants and not on your bare behind. Not this time anyway.'

'Ooh, it still stings a bit!' Dylan said, his butt cheeks tantalizingly shaking a little.

'It's meant to,' Flint countered back. 'And is that boner getting even harder inside your pants? There will be trouble if there is. Believe me.'

Dylan didn't respond.

Flint could quite clearly feel Dylan's dick growing and throbbing the more Flint spanked him.

This needed seeing to.

There was *no way* Flint was going to let this slide.

He had to show Dylan exactly who was boss.

And what happened when his orders were disobeyed.

There was only one Daddy Dom in this relationship, and that was Flint.

Of course, the fact that Flint was turned on was a factor too.

Dylan's perfect little butt was equal parts adorable and extremely sexy.

It was small.

Yet very peachy.

Perfect for spanking.

Incredibly desirable.

'I can feel your dick pressing up against me,' Dylan said. 'It feels... massive!'

'Enough!' Flint bellowed. 'Enough sass. You need to be taught a lesson, Little!'

With that, Flint rolled Dylan off his lap.

Towering over him, and with his own bulge hugely prominent at the front of his pants, Flint was in no mood for messing around.

It was time to take Dylan's discipline to the next level.

Chapter Thirteen

I can't believe how hot he looks.

Standing over me.

I feel so helpless, at his mercy...

There was no disputing how aroused Dylan felt.

It had been a great morning. From the initial feeling of wholesomeness waking up next to Flint to the surprise of Flint taking the morning off work.

And things had only got better from there too.

Dylan had enjoyed his breakfast and then the coloring and drawing session that had followed.

It hadn't taken much, but for the first time in a long time Dylan had found himself in his Little Space.

His mind was perfectly contented.

At peace.

Totally happy and just going with the flow.

It was like a dream.

And then to see Flint getting involved in his playing too. It had been the definition of perfection. Dylan knew it wasn't easy for Flint to play with stuffies. But the way Flint made the effort and gradually got into it was brilliant.

It made Dylan feel ever so grateful for having found Flint.

Even if it was in such terrible circumstances.

Talk about a silver lining.

Of course, the way the situation had developed was pretty lovely too.

Suddenly, Dylan had found himself being spanked and then rolled onto the floor.

His dick hard.

His Daddy's dick just as hard. And a lot bigger too.

Dylan was in awe of Flint's physicality. There was something so arousing about his testosterone fueled masculinity.

It made Dylan feel so submissive.

Exactly how he liked to feel.

It was a big part of his identity as a Little.

Dylan needed a big, strong Daddy who wasn't afraid to be firm and physical.

Flint very much fit this description.

In a big way.

And now, at Flint's feet, Dylan was about to find out exactly what his Daddy had in store for him next...

'I think you enjoyed that spanking a little bit too much,' Flint bellowed, his voice sounding as imperious and commanding as ever. 'I'm going to have to take matters into my own hands. It's time to teach you a lesson you will not forget in a hurry.'

Dylan's heart began to thump even harder inside his chest.

Dylan was turned on.

But he was also a little bit scared too.

In a good way.

Flint was super-intense, but it was a major turn on for

Dylan.

'Y-y-y-yes, Daddy,' Dylan said, his senses on high alert. 'I'll do anything you say.'

Without saying another word, Flint hauled Dylan up onto his feet and then slung him over his shoulder.

Dylan gasped as he felt Flint yank his pants down off his ass and onto his ankles.

'Still hard. Oh dear, that's an extra ten thwacks,' Flint said, feeling Dylan's now exposed boner press against his shoulder.

'*Gulp!*' Dylan said, giggling a little bit.

He was ready for more punishment and if anything, actually wanted to provoke Flint a little bit.

'Keep the sass up,' Flint responded. 'We'll see how cocky you are in a minute.'

The way Flint said those words made Dylan slightly regret being so sassy

He was at Flint's mercy.

It might have been a better idea to take the punishment without trying to be bratty.

But it was too late now.

Before Dylan knew what was happening, Flint had lowered him to the ground and was putting Dylan's hands inside some handcuffs.

'Police issue, the real thing,' Flint said. 'So don't even think about trying to break out of them. These are about as far from plastic toy cuffs as you can get.'

Dylan stood submissively as Flint tore his t-shirt off his body.

It was *thrilling*.

Dylan could see that Flint was in full-on Daddy Dom mode.

Nothing was going to stop him giving Dylan the punishment he needed.

'What if I try to run? My legs aren't cuffed!' Dylan said, the words spilling out of his mouth as the adrenalin pumped over his whole body. 'I'm pretty speedy. Especially when up against an older cop like you!'

Flint had a look of pure rage on his face.

Dylan was pushing him to his limits.

'Try running now,' Flint barked, swiftly attaching the cuffs to the metal headboard at the top of the bed. 'Go on. Try it. Ha! You're trapped. And you're all mine.'

Dylan gulped as he saw what Flint was doing.

Flint opened the large cupboard across from the bed and took out what appeared to be the flattest, swishiest paddle imaginable.

Suddenly, Dylan was scared.

He'd never been paddled before and the reality of it was hitting home.

And hard.

But not as hard as the paddle would.

'Please, go easy on me! I'll do anything you want,' Dylan pleaded, his words not being heeded.

'Too late. Too much sass. *Way* too much sass,' Flint said, letting out a menacing chuckle. 'It's time to paddle this butt until you learn exactly who the boss is.'

Flint proceeded to bring the paddle down on Dylan's cheeks.

Within seconds, Dylan was yelping and crying out in pain.

Flint was an expert paddler.

Of course he was.

He could land blows on each cheek, or right in the middle of both.

Each swat was hard, fast, and accurate.

Flint didn't miss his intended target once.

And Dylan quickly realized that his Daddy was not to be messed with.

Flint was a true Daddy Dom, there was absolutely no room for doubt.

'Have you learned your lesson yet?' Flint bellowed, definitely enjoying the sight of Dylan's glowing cheeks wobble as he brought down another swat of the paddle.

'I have! I have!' Dylan pleaded.

This hurts so bad.

But it feels so good too...

Dylan was equally in pain and turned on. Having never been paddled before, Dylan had been nervous beforehand. But under the expert tutelage of Flint, Dylan was learning that he was more than capable of taking a paddling.

After one final swish of the paddle, it was over.

'Good. You took that well. Not perfectly, but excellent for a first timer,' Flint said, resting the paddle down on the bed. 'But don't think this is over. It isn't. Not even close.'

'I-I-I-I don't think my butt can take much more,' Dylan said, his voice wavering a little.

'Don't worry, it's not your ass I'm after this time,' Flint said, a smile on his face.

Flint unhooked the cuffs from the bedpost bet kept the handcuffs on Dylan.

'On your knees,' Flint commanded. 'Now.'

Dylan did exactly as he was told.

It felt freeing to not even question Flint's instructions.

Just follow them like a good sub.

Exactly like a good Little should when instructed by their Daddy.

Flint proceeded to remove his rock-hard dick from his pants.

Dylan gasped as he saw Flint's meat bounce out. It was hard. Veiny. And very, *very* long.

Dylan had a feeling he knew what Flint wanted next.

But he knew he had to wait for Flint to give him his instructions before he could do anything.

This was about learning who was in charge.

As much as Dylan wanted to get to work on Flint's cock, he had to show that he was a disciplined Little.

'Good. Don't let temptation get the better of you,' Flint said, his voice even and with a hint of friendliness to it. 'Now you may begin. I want you to work that mouth of yours up and down. All the way. Show me how well you can suck your master's dick.'

Dylan nodded.

Without a second's pause, he placed his lips on the tip of Flint's bulbous head and began to kiss it.

Slowly at first, but then with increasing speed, Dylan began to work his tongue over Flint's wide dick head.

Soon, he was easing his mouth down the shaft.

It was thick and long.

Hard to take at first.

Soon enough though, Dylan was bobbing his head up and down. The sound of Flint's moans and grunts drove Dylan on to use his tongue more, go deeper, show Flint what he was capable of.

'Faster!' Flint decreed, grabbing Dylan's head and assisting Dylan with his blow job.

It felt hot to be used like this.

Dylan knew it was an intimate act. Just between the two of them. Dylan knew that Flint cared deeply for him. It was okay to act out the fantasy of being a sex object.

As Flint continued to grunt and Dylan coughed and spluttered at the sheer size of Flint's manhood, Dylan felt Flint's muscles tensing.

He wasn't far off cumming.

'When I let my load loose, you take it all in your mouth,' Flint said, his breathing heavy. 'You swallow it down too. Don't waste a single drop.'

Dylan tried to answer, but it was difficult with a mouth full of Flint's dick.

As Flint filled Dylan's mouth up with salty, thick cum, Dylan did exactly as he was told and swallowed it all.

The taste was strong.

The texture was a lot to handle.

But there was no doubt in Dylan's mind about following Flint's orders. It was sexy to do what he was told in this situation. Dylan wouldn't have changed it for anything in the world.

* * *

Dylan let out a satisfied sigh as Flint washed his body with a hot flannel in the bath.

Their roleplay had been intense.

A lot of fun, but *very* tiring.

'Was everything good for you?' Flint said. 'Remember you can always say if there was something you weren't into so much.'

'No, I loved it all Daddy,' Dylan said. 'Even the hardest of the hard swats! I've never been paddled before, but I would like to be again.'

'Don't worry, you will be soon enough,' Flint chuckled, washing the shampoo out of Dylan's hair. 'All done. Time for bed for you. And for me too. I'm beat. We both deserve a daytime nap. It's surprising how tiring a day off can be, right?'

Dylan giggled.

They had done an awful lot over the day, and it wasn't even lunch time.

Flint took Dylan out of the bath and dried him off using one of his over-sized extra-fluffy towels. Dylan felt tiny inside the towel. And he just loved the way that Flint wrapped him up inside it and carried him through to the bedroom.

The pair of them got into bed and snuggled up to each other.

Flint was the big spoon of course.

Dylan hadn't had an orgasm but felt totally satisfied.

Maybe this was part of Flint's orgasm denial thing?

Dylan didn't have long to contemplate that though, his eyes slowly closed and he found himself falling in to a deep, deep sleep.

* * *

Dylan woke up from the nap to the sound of Flint's snores.

A couple of hours had passed.

Dylan looked across the bed and saw that Flint was showing no signs of waking up. Not even a single movement to suggest it.

Dylan suddenly had an idea.

As nice as it was to have all of the toys and stuffies that Flint had ordered, Dylan was missing his own.

Especially his number one stuffie, Pinky.

Dylan decided to sneak out of the apartment and head back to his own place to collect Pinky.

He could be there and back before Flint woke up.

On some level, Dylan felt like he shouldn't be considering it. But he figured that he could do it so quickly it would save time in the long run. And leave more time for him and Flint to hang out together.

Dylan quietly snuck out of bed, got dressed and headed over to his apartment. The traffic was pretty quiet and as the Uber dropped him off outside the building, Dylan took a quick look around.

Just in case he spotted any unsavory characters.

It didn't feel very good to be back at his building.

The memories of what had happened were still way too raw.

But Dylan was here for one thing, and one thing only.

Pinky.

Up in the apartment, Dylan immediately located Pinky on his bed and picked him up.

'I've missed you! You're going to love Flint's apartment, I just know you will,' Dylan said, giving Pinky the biggest cuddle ever. '*Hmm*, what's this?'

Dylan walked over and saw his Nintendo Switch.

He couldn't resist.

Dylan sat down with Pinky and loaded up a quick game.

He figured he was there now, one or two games wouldn't take long. And when he was done, he could take the Switch with him back to Flint's.

But one or two games turned into ten or fifteen.

Without Dylan realizing, a whole two hours had passed.

It was at this moment in time that a furious Flint burst into the apartment, shocking Dylan to his core.

'What the fuck do you call this?' Flint said, his voice full of anger. 'I cannot believe you put yourself in danger like this. I am absolutely livid. This is not on. It is entirely unacceptable behavior that will not be tolerated.'

Dylan didn't know what to say.

He had been caught red handed.

Dylan also knew that Flint was right. He shouldn't have left the apartment without saying anything. Deep down, Dylan knew full well that Flint wouldn't have allowed him to go. That was why he'd snuck out.

There was a look in Flint's face that told Dylan he wasn't messing around.

All Dylan could do was hope that his punishment wasn't going to be too painful.

But Flint wasn't done talking yet.

'I will not accept you leaving the apartment and coming here,' Flint said, pacing up and down the room. 'It's ridiculous I should have to say it. And, yes, your punishment will be severe. I have no other choice. Not now. Trust me, when you're done you'll never disobey me and do something silly like this again.'

'Yes, Daddy,' Dylan said, his voice wavering a bit as he realized how foolish he had been. 'I'm sorry.'

Dylan was trying hard not to burst into tears.

He knew he had badly let himself down.

And his Daddy too.

This feeling sucked.

Sucked big time.

'Enough!' Flint barked. 'Don't give me any of that nonsense. You did what you did and now it's time to pay the price. I don't like this any more than you will, but you've left me absolutely no choice. Brace yourself. You're not going to like what's coming next.'

Oh no, is Flint going to break up with me?

Zack Wish

Did I just make the worst mistake of my whole life?
I'm scared. I don't like this at all...

Chapter Fourteen

When Flint had woken up to find that Dylan was neither in bed, nor in the apartment either, he had freaked out.

Flint was terrified.

Anything could have happened to Dylan.

It wasn't safe for him out there in the world alone.

Not while that pervert stalker was still out on the loose.

In a furious rush, Flint had put his clothes on and made his way to Dylan's apartment.

It was instinct.

Call it his *Detective's Intuition.*

But Flint had known that Dylan would head back there.

Flint had recalled Dylan talking about his favorite stuffie, Pinky. It would be enough to make him sneak out. Flint just knew it.

He used Dylan's spare key to enter the apartment and the sight of Dylan sitting on his couch playing on a games console was a huge relief.

It also made Flint nearly hit the roof in anger.

After exploding into a rage, Flint gathered himself.

He needed to punish Dylan for this, but it had to be something appropriate.

It needed to be a punishment that would focus Dylan's mind on the task at hand and make him not ever want to repeat offend again.

'Okay, here's the situation,' Flint said. 'You're not going to get a paddling or spanking. Far too enjoyable. No. What you need is the kind of punishment that won't stimulate you in that way. Not even close.'

Flint could see that Dylan was listening intently.

He could also see that Dylan had absolutely no idea as to what was coming his way.

'You will be doing lines. Old school, handwritten lines,' Flint said, showing no emotion. 'And you will do them to the highest standard. Not a single letter out of place. Neatly written. Total accuracy and discipline on each and every letter.'

Dylan looked aghast.

Flint smiled internally but maintained his gruff exterior.

Dylan had to know that Flint wasn't messing around.

'H-h-h-h-how many lines?' Dylan asked, twiddling with his fingers nervously. 'I haven't done lines since school. I used to hate them!'

'Good, I'm glad to hear that,' Flint said. 'Perhaps this will teach you then to not do such foolish things. I think two hundred lines should suffice.'

'Two hundred! But—'

'No buts,' Flint said, slamming his palm down onto the messy side-table. 'You will do the two hundred lines. You will do them flawlessly. If I spot a single mistake, you will go right back to the start and repeat the entire process. I don't care if that is after nine lines or one hundred and ninety-nine. Understood?'

Dylan nodded solemnly.

The message had hit home.

That was good to see.

'You will write *I must always tell Daddy where I am*. Do I need to say it again?' Flint asked, staring at Dylan with his sternest Daddy Dom expression.

'No, Daddy,' Dylan said, crestfallen. 'I understand.'

'Very good. Now fetch yourself your neatest lined paper and a pen. I want to see you sitting at this table and making a start in sixty seconds flat.'

'Yes, Daddy,' Dylan replied, quickly scurrying to find his smartest writing paper and pen. 'I'm sorry. I'm so, so sorry.'

'Silence!' Flint said, not interested in any more talking. 'Get to work.'

Dylan wasted no time and began writing his lines.

Flint paced around Dylan's apartment, looking for something he might have missed when investigating the stalker.

Nothing.

Not even the slightest hint of a previously unearthed clue.

This was frustrating.

Meanwhile, Flint listened as Dylan huffed and puffed.

'Writing lines isn't meant to be fun,' Flint said. 'That's the whole point of them. Now be quiet and concentrate on getting them right.'

The truth was, Flint wasn't enjoying this punishment.

There was no pleasure in it for either him or Dylan.

But that wasn't the point, of course.

This was all about Dylan learning a valuable life lesson.

Personal safety mattered.

As did responsibility.

And above all, listening to his Daddy was important.

'My hand hurts,' Dylan said, sounding very fed-up and over writing lines. 'It's sore Daddy and I've still got another hundred to go.'

'Well, you can rest your hand when you're done,' Flint said, outwardly showing no emotion but feeling empathy for Dylan. 'Keep it up, young man. I'll be here from you when you're done.'

Dylan smiled.

It wasn't exactly a smile of sheer joy, but it showed Flint that Dylan was listening to his words and taking them on board.

The truth was that Dylan was beginning to mean an awful lot to Flint.

Yes, Flint thought Dylan was super-cute.

Yes, he loved spanking his butt.

And, yes, the blowjob had been superb.

But the connection Flint felt ran much deeper than anything sexual.

Over the last few days, Flint had seen first-hand and close up just how brilliant and unique an individual Dylan was.

He was one of a kind.

A Little worth holding close and protecting at all costs.

Flint felt honored to be his Daddy.

Flint stopped pacing around and took a seat next to Dylan as he carried on conscientiously writing his lines.

'You know, I think of you very highly,' Flint said, resting his hand on Dylan's non-writing hand. 'We haven't been together long, but I can sense our bond is like we've been Daddy and Little for so much longer. It feels special. Very special. I hope you feel the same.'

Dylan nodded.

'I do,' Dylan said. 'I definitely feel the same. Now quit distracting me, Daddy. I've got two hundred lines to finish!'

Flint chuckled.

'That's the spirit,' Flint said. 'Keep your chin up and your eyes on the prize. Not long to go now. The last stretch will fly by.'

While it didn't exactly fly by, Dylan's final few lines passed without too much drama.

Flint felt proud that Dylan took so much pride in making sure that his work was completed to a high standard. Not only did it show Flint that his instructions were being taken seriously, but it also bode well for Dylan's future acting plans.

Dylan had talent.

And now it looked like he was developing discipline too.

'You know, your safety is my paramount concern,' Flint said as he poured Dylan a glass of tap water. 'I'll do anything to protect you. *Always*. But you have to learn to trust me when I speak. If I say something is a no-go, you listen. Does that make sense?'

'It does, Daddy,' Dylan said.

Dylan thanked Flint for the water and took a couple of sips before carrying on with the lines.

He was nearly done now.

Not many left to do.

Then, disaster.

Dylan lost control of his pen for a split-second and made a blunder on his lettering. He looked horrified.

Then, to Flint's surprise, Dylan steadied himself.

'Daddy, I think I need to start again,' Dylan said. 'I lost concentration and wrote a letter messily. Please can I have another sheet of paper to go again from the beginning?'

Flint was bowled over with how well Dylan owned his error.

This was impressive.

Seriously mature behavior from his Little.

But Flint decided to surprise Dylan.

'No, that won't be necessary,' Flint said. 'Carry on and finish up the remaining lines. One mistake doesn't ruin everything. I think we can both agree on that.'

'Are you sure, Daddy?'

'Hey, don't question my generosity, I might change my mind!'

Dylan smiled and beavered away on his final lines until it was all done. When he was finished, Dylan handed the sheet to Flint for a closer inspection.

'This is good. It's actually superb,' Flint mused, scanning his eyes across all two hundred lines. 'Excellent lettering. Flawless spelling. No signs of rushing or lack of care. You've done yourself proud here, kiddo.'

Dylan smiled a big smile.

He was proud of himself.

Flint could tell that the lesson had very much be learned.

That was all he needed to see.

The one small mistake wasn't a big deal at all. It was actually a blessing as it had given Dylan the chance to show his maturity and offer to start over. That hadn't been necessary. The success of the task was abundantly clear.

Flint offered his hand and gently lifted Dylan to his feet.

Wrapping his heavy hands around Dylan's tight waist, Flint brought Dylan in toward his body and they began to kiss.

It was a hot, heavy kiss.

The kind of passion that can very easily spill over into more.

'Here? Now?' Flint said, grabbing Dylan's crotch and squeezing his hardening bulge.

Dylan nodded, moving his own hands underneath Flint's t-shirt and running his dainty fingers over Flint's toned stomach and rock-hard pecs.

'Yes please!' Dylan said, seemingly thrilled at the prospect of his punishment segueing into something altogether more pleasure oriented.

The pair continued to kiss.

It was a struggle for Flint to not tear off Dylan's clothes and take him right there on the spot.

Dylan had even turned around and was grinding his perfectly round ass into Flint's engorged dick.

This was heading one way, and one way only.

Then, out of the blue, Dylan's phone began to flash and ping.

'*Urgh*, who the hell is that?' Flint said, frustrated at the distraction.

'Who cares, I'll leave it,' Dylan said, panting.

'*Grrr*. No. You can't do that,' Flint replied, firmly moving Dylan away from him. 'It could be something important. We can always pick up where we left off soon enough. You know me. The master of orgasm control.'

Flint was a lot more frustrated than he was letting on.

He had very much been into it.

He wanted things to go further than they ever had.

But, at the same time it wouldn't look good if after a punishment relating to discipline, Flint let Dylan ignore a potentially important message.

Flint knew all too well from his own life experiences coming up through the ranks of the NYPD that every day a lesson was learned, and there would soon be a further test just around the corner.

The key was consistency.

That was how true learning was done.

'Fine,' Dylan said, pouting a little bit. 'You win!'

His face flushed red from arousal, Flint watched as Dylan walked over towards his phone.

There was a pause as Dylan picked up his cell phone to read the message.

Flint was worried.

Was it another image from the stalker?

That wouldn't be good news at all.

Maybe it had been a mistake to spend a single second longer in the apartment than they had needed.

'Talk to me, Dylan,' Flint said, his voice full of concern.

Dylan put the phone down on the table and looked at Flint.

Flint tried to gauge what Dylan was feeling in that moment, but it wasn't easy.

He just needed Dylan to speak.

Tell him what the hell was going on.

'Yes?' Flint said, impatiently. 'Speak!'

'Daddy,' Dylan replied. 'You're not going to believe who that message was from, or what they had to say...'

Chapter Fifteen

Dylan had felt incredibly nervous as he picked up his cell phone to read the message.

For all he knew, it could have been from the same creep who had sent him the photos.

In fact, a part of Dylan had strongly suspected that this was exactly who the message might have been from.

So it was to his huge relief when he picked up the phone and saw something altogether different.

Different and unexpected.

In a good way, thankfully.

Much to Dylan's shock, the message was an email from a romance author. It was a romance author who Dylan had only recently discovered. They were relatively new but quickly gathering a large following.

But what did they want?

In a state of shock, Dylan skim-read the email once and then went right back to the beginning to read it all over again.

Was the author being serious?

'Come on, tell me what the message is,' Flint said, breaking Dylan out of his trance-like state.

'It's a romance author, one I really like,' Dylan said, still struggling to comprehend the offer that had been made. 'They want me to narrate their DDlb book!'

Flint looked stunned.

Dylan felt the same.

But in an instant, the pair of them had rushed over to each other and were hugging.

'This is brilliant news, I'm so proud of you!' Flint said, a generosity and warmth in his voice that made Dylan feel all gooey inside. 'Seriously, this is superb. Totally incredible.'

Dylan felt like he could cry.

Tears of joy though, not sadness.

It felt like his life was turning around.

Something that only a few short days ago felt like an impossibility.

First Flint, and now the audiobook offer.

Everything was coming up Dylan.

'Should I email them back right now?' Dylan said, his voice bubbling over with excitement to the extent that he could hardly get his words out. 'I mean, I want to. But I don't want to come off as desperate?'

Flint smiled.

'Relax. You're good. Yes, reply now,' Flint said. 'The author made you the offer. They approached *you*. You have nothing to worry about. Be enthusiastic. It goes a long way.'

Dylan was grateful for Flint's advice.

He had so much more life experience.

And a successful career to back it up too.

Plus, Flint knew the ways of the world so much more than Dylan.

In fact, it was like he was straight out of a dream Daddy playbook.

Dylan typed out a response to the author and hit the send button. This was incredibly exciting.

Was his career about to take off?

Certainly, the financial reward was good.

But more than that, it was the fact that someone wanted him for their special project. They were willing to trust his voice acting skills with the novel that they had spent many a long hour working on.

'I guess it was worth uploading my voice samples onto all those voice talent websites, right?' Dylan said. 'Another great recommendation. How can I repay you, Daddy?'

Dylan blushed a little as many rude and naughty thoughts crossed his mind.

Evidently, Flint was thinking along the same lines...

'Trust me, I'll think of *plenty* of ways,' Flint said with a devilishly mischievous smile. 'You can bank on that.'

'*Hehe*, I believe you,' Dylan said, his mind racing.

Dylan suddenly found his mind pulled back in the direction of the audiobook narration offer.

'Daddy, would you mind if I made a start on it now?' Dylan said. 'I want to send some character samples over to the author. You know, really show how professional I am. Who knows, it could be the start of a long working relationship.'

Flint made a thumbs up sign with both thumbs.

Very cheesy Daddy behavior, but Dylan didn't mind.

Dylan could see that this turn of events had made Flint proud of him. It was a *superb* feeling.

It wasn't long ago when Dylan didn't think he would ever find a good Daddy. Certainly not one who would devote so much of their time and energy into nurturing and looking after him like Flint was doing.

Those kinds of qualities were rare.

As far as Dylan's own experience had gone, they were practically unheard of.

Almost mythical in quality, like unicorns.

But what was happening now was very much grounded in reality. And it was down in a large part to Flint.

Flint looked like he was taking a moment to consider something.

Dylan figured Flint might have been assessing whether it was safe or not to leave him alone at the apartment.

'Um, yeah, you go for it,' Flint said. 'Knock it out of the park, kid.'

'Yay! I'll try, Daddy,' Dylan said, already opening up his laptop and loading up the recording software. 'Thanks again for helping with, you know... *everything*.'

'Hey, you'll do great,' Flint said. 'And thanks, I appreciate that. But you're the talent. You just needed a helpful nudge. Or should that be spank?'

The pair of them laughed.

'Okay, time for me to head down to the station,' Flint said. 'Crime doesn't solve itself. Trust me on that.'

'If anyone can solve all the cases, it's you Daddy.'

After a brief goodbye cuddle and kiss, Flint exited.

Dylan heard the apartment door shut and began recording. It was time to get down to things.

Dylan was slowly learning the software.

It wasn't the easiest system to get a hold of, but Dylan knew that practice would make perfect.

'Hey, Pinky, that sounds like something Flint would say, doesn't it?' Dylan joked, casting his glance over to the ever loyal stuffie. 'I know, I know. We're super-duper lucky to have him.'

After a bit of fiddling around on the software, Dylan finally got into recording some character samples.

It was fun to get into the heads of the characters, especially the main Little. The lead Little actually had a lot in common with Dylan, and this made really capturing his spirit so much fun and rewarding.

Dylan began to see a real future for himself doing this.

It surprised him just how much he enjoyed it.

Okay, it wasn't a lead role on Broadway in the kind of show he had dreamed of for so long.

But it was something.

Dylan was being a free thinker, letting his creative juices flow.

It was very exciting to be voicing the creations of an author he admired. Dylan had never even considered this side of writing, but when he thought of it there were so many audiobook versions of his favorite romance books.

Someone had to voice them.

So why couldn't it be him?

Well, now it was him!

One of the plot points of the novel involved the Little character having their heart broken by a cruel Daddy. Definitely not the character's Forever Daddy and certainly not a keeper in any sense.

Dylan took a brief break.

It was quite intense being in this headspace and he couldn't help but think back to how his old Daddy had been such a horrible guy in the end.

Yuck, what a jerk.

I hate thinking about him.

But maybe I can use that emotion for good...

Finishing off his raspberry and apple juice box, Dylan put his headphones back on and got back to work.

Using the pain he went through because of his horrible former Daddy, he channeled it into the Little character in the romance novel.

It worked.

In fact, the results felt spectacular to Dylan.

He finished a brief monologue and hit stop on the recording.

'Wow, Pinky. I think I nailed it!' Dylan said, leaning back in his chair. '*Hmmm*. Still giving me the silent treatment. Okay, let's have a break and eat some sweet treats, shall we?'

Pinky yet again maintained his silence.

But Dylan was more than happy to assume Pinky wanted a treat as much as he did.

Armed with a big jar of cookies with extra sprinkles on top, Dylan walked with Pinky and took a seat on his couch.

He'd been recording for over an hour and needed a break.

It was super-tiring.

He figured the more he did it, the greater his stamina would get.

But for today, this was a great beginning.

As Dylan crunched away on a cookie, he saw his cell-phone flash up with a message from his fellow Little and BFF, Casper.

Hey! How's the recording going? I was thinking, if I do an audio version of the webcomic you should definitely do the voices. Imagine how super-duper-magic that would be? Anyway, gotta go. I have a date! Casper XoXo

. . .

Dylan typed out a reply and did it with a big smile on his face. It felt superb to have been invited to get involved with Casper's professional life.

Casper was a very talented and successful comic maker. He had a large following online and a well-supported Patreon too.

Being able to combine their personal and professional lives could be a whole lot of fun. There was no doubting that.

After finishing up his break, Dylan got back down to business.

It took him only a few moments to get back into the swing of the recording. The software was beginning to feel a lot easier to use and Dylan was having a lot of fun experimenting with the character voices while at the same time also working on his more controlled general narration.

It felt like fun.

But it was a paid job.

Dylan couldn't have asked for anymore.

After finishing off one block of dialogue, Dylan heard the apartment door open.

It must have been Flint returning from work.

He'd probably forgotten something.

'I'm still recording but come and say hi!' Dylan shouted cheerily, his big headphones muffling the sounds of the apartment a little bit.

There was no reply from Flint.

'Hey, Daddy! Come over here, I want to show you this cool new pitch tool. I can make myself sound like a chipmunk!' Dylan shouted.

Still no response from Flint.

It was at that moment a chill came over Dylan.

What was taking Flint so long to come over and greet him?

Dylan took his headphones off and called out once more.

This time there was a response.

A voice.

But it wasn't Flint's gruff Daddy voice.

It was someone else.

Someone else was in the apartment.

But who?

The floorboards creaked as the other person got closer to Dylan.

Dylan suddenly felt terrified.

He gripped Pinky and held his stuffie close.

Dylan was trapped and had no idea what on earth he was meant to do next.

I wish Flint was here.

I need my Daddy now more than ever...

Chapter Sixteen

Flint couldn't decide whether to have a glazed donut or stick to his selection of nuts.

One healthy option versus a sugary treat.

Flint knew for sure which option Dylan would select.

Obviously, the sugary donut.

Flint even considered texting Dylan for his advice.

But he thought better of it as he didn't want to disturb him and his recordings.

Flint felt another swell of pride as he considered just how well Dylan had done. Although Flint didn't know much about how the industry worked, he knew it was a big deal to get asked to record for an up-and-coming romance author.

It was still very new.

The feeling of having a connection with someone on the Daddy and Little level. Flint had been worried that he was too cynical, not well enough adjusted to be a good influence. To be the right type of personality that a Little needed.

But so far, it actually appeared that Flint's fears had been misplaced.

Dylan seemed to be going from strength to strength.

But it wasn't just Dylan who had benefitted from their relationship.

Flint was feeling better about himself too.

There was the satisfaction he felt from stepping into Dylan's life and providing him with safety, security, and something resembling normality.

Especially after what Dylan had recently been through.

But even taking the stalker situation into account, Flint felt like Dylan's life had still been missing the stability that a Daddy could bring.

Alongside the warm feeling of knowing he was helping someone else, Flint had felt himself open up and relax a bit too. He never would have considered calling in sick before.

In fact, he'd gone into work many times over the years feeling like absolute trash.

Determined not to miss a single morning.

Flint had even cancelled tooth surgery to avoid missing a shift.

Taking a slight step back from work didn't come easy to him.

Far from it.

But it was a little bit easier now he was with Dylan.

It was like he had a concrete reason to put at least some of his energies into something other than solving cases and grinding away at his enormous backlog of police work.

'Okay, I'm going for the donut, screw it,' Flint said, laughing with a colleague as the pair of them each grabbed two donuts each and emptied the box. 'One of the new guys can haul ass and re-fill these later.'

Flint walked back to his desk.

After munching down the donuts, Flint found it a struggle to keep his head in the work. It might have been the gargantuan stack of paperwork to his right, or the similarly large stack of work to his left, but he just could *not* focus.

The aircon was also struggling to maintain any kind of consistency. And what made it worse was that not only was it not cooling the office, but it was also making intermittent loud thudding and whirring noises.

'Shut that fucking thing up!' Detective Kal Brasenose shouted.

Kal was sitting a few desks away from Flint.

They weren't exactly best buddies, but on the subject of the faltering aircon both could agree that something needed to be done.

'I hear that,' Flint replied, his frustration growing.

Deep down, Flint knew that he didn't want to be in work at all.

Faulty aircon or not.

Where he wanted to be was with Dylan.

But there was work to be done at the station. There was no getting around that. Flint began to slowly plough his way through the outstanding paperwork.

Progress was slow.

Flint even decided to put in his special noise cancelling earbuds. This wasn't something he liked to do often, and it was definitely frowned upon by his boss who saw it as very anti-social.

But if there was any hope of Flint concentrating, he knew he would need to cancel out as much of the surrounding distractions as possible.

The earbuds worked for a while.

But it wasn't long before Flint's mind began to wander again.

Flint couldn't help but think back to his old partner, Mickie.

It had been a vice bust. Nothing out of the ordinary. Or so they thought. But when Mickie and Flint were ambushed, it turned into a total nightmare. One that sadly Mickie would never wake from.

Despite managing to escape the ambush, Mickie had taken several bullets. He managed to cling on to life for long enough for Flint to get them both to the hospital and into the emergency operating theater.

After that, everything went downhill.

Mickie's body just couldn't handle the trauma.

As he passed away in the early hours of that morning, something in Flint changed.

Changed forever.

Up until that point, Flint had been utterly fearless and relentless. He had no fear of any situation on the tough streets. Flint had taken down more bad guys in hand-to-hand combat than he could count.

But losing Mickie in such a brutal way was an eye-opener.

It took a long time for Flint to get his head around the whole situation.

Flint's mind was plagued with thoughts that it had been his fault. That he could have done something – *anything* – differently. That if he had made a different move, Mickie would still be alive today.

Flint's sergeant had seen it all before.

Experienced it himself.

That's why he initially allowed Flint to deal with the grief in his own way. Sergeant Mase gave Flint space.

Maybe *too much* space.

It led to Flint slowly withdrawing from the social side of

the police force. He rarely went out for drinks or socialized with his fellow cops anymore.

Flint could feel himself slowly slipping into introspection.

Police work wasn't as enjoyable any longer.

It hurt him.

Not as bad as the pain of losing Mickie, but more like a slow-burn pain. The kind that just nags away at an individual.

The end result was that Flint just didn't work the beat any longer. He had no one to walk the streets with. He simply wasn't interested in having another partner.

Why would he be?

The risk of going through the agony of losing a partner all over again just wasn't something that Flint could even contemplate.

No, he decided he would do police work his way.

And that meant staying behind the desk for as much of the time as he possibly could. Flint would go to crime scenes as and when required of course. That was unavoidable and a huge part of solving any case.

But as far as walking the beat went?

No chance.

Flint was done with that.

Well, that was what he'd always assumed. Since spending time with Dylan and seeing how change was possible, Flint had begun to very gradually thaw to the idea of hitting the streets again.

It wouldn't be easy.

There were still major psychological hoops for Flint to jump through. He considered that maybe it was time to see a therapist to talk over Mickie's death. Maybe even ask for an extended period off work to focus on himself and return as the cop he knew he once was. The cop who he prayed he could be again.

But Flint figured that if he could keep Dylan safe, then perhaps he could trust himself to do the same with the good people of New York City again.

With his mood lifted, a sense of genuine optimism came over Flint.

He used this energy to make a decent dent in the stack of work on his desk. It wasn't like he'd got anywhere near clearing it, but he absolutely got through more than he normally would.

It was like his old efficiency and gut instinct was trying to get out. One step at a time. Slowly but surely.

Flint even got a compliment of Sergeant Mase.

This was a rare occurrence.

Mase was tough. Old school.

When Mase said something was good, you knew he meant it.

So, it was with something of a spring in his step that Flint finished off his last case file for the day and headed out onto the sweltering streets outside the station.

It had been a long day's work.

But ultimately a satisfying one.

Flint was planning on heading directly back to Dylan's apartment without stopping. But then he had an idea. It was time to treat Dylan as a reward for all of his hard work.

But it wasn't going to be a sweet treat.

No, Dylan didn't need any more sugary snacks.

Flint was going to surprise Dylan with a brand-new paddle.

One that would be perfect for dishing out a blistering spanking the next time Dylan acted a little bit too bratty for his own good.

Or if Dylan applied too much sass.

Or if... well, it wasn't going to take much of an excuse for Flint to spank him.

Flint felt confident that Dylan would be very much on board with this surprise. The spanking supplies store was only a couple of blocks detour. Flint figured that Dylan would be more than happy to wait a little bit longer before he got home.

Briefly taking a moment to get his bearings, Flint wasted no more time considering it. It was time to pick up a new paddle and then head over to see Dylan.

Flint hopped out of the Uber and looked up towards Dylan's apartment window.

The new paddle was safely hidden inside Flint's work bag. He wanted it to be as much of a surprise as possible and had been considering ways he could let Dylan in on the secret in the most fun way imaginable.

There were plenty of options.

Flint even considered marching into the apartment and dishing out a big old paddling right there and then.

He figured he would make his mind up when he saw Dylan.

After all, if Dylan was still working then it wouldn't be a very Daddy thing to do to distract Dylan away from his responsibilities.

That was the last thing Flint wanted.

Flint entered the building and made his way up the stairs. Naturally, the elevator was out of order. This was typical of the building. Poorly managed and in need of a new owner.

Still, if it gave Flint a chance to work off some of the donut-calories from earlier, he wasn't going to complain too much.

As Flint approached Dylan's apartment, he felt something.

It was the kind of sickening feeling he got when working a fresh case.

Something was up.

The atmosphere was off.

Every single one of Flint's cop instincts kicked in.

Adrenalin pumped around his body.

Flint ran towards the apartment door and noticed that it was off its hinges.

'What the fuck!' Flint said, panic in his voice. 'Dylan! Dylan! Are you okay? Where are you? Answer me!'

Flint charged into the apartment, but Dylan was nowhere to be seen.

There was no sign of a struggle.

It didn't look like anything had been messed around with.

Barely a single item was out of place.

But the door...

'Fuck, fuck, fuck!' Flint raged. 'Dylan!'

It was a shout of exasperation.

Dylan wasn't there and the truth was that he had almost certainly been taken. There was no other explanation for the door being off the hinges.

Flint was terrified.

Dylan meant absolutely *everything* to him.

They may not have been together for long, but the bond between them was true.

Flint was Dylan's Daddy.

And there was no way in hell that Flint was going to let anything happen to him.

Not today, and not ever.

It was time for Detective Flint Maddox to hit the streets once more.

Chapter Seventeen

Dylan felt so scared.

More scared than at any other point in his life.

He didn't know where he was.

All he knew was that he absolutely hated it.

'*Hmph*, can't you get that miserable look off your face?'

'W-w-w-who are you?' Dylan said, looking over at the man who had kidnapped him. 'Just let me go. I pinky-promise I won't tell anyone. Not the police. Not my friends. No one.'

'You don't recognize me? It's me, Tommy,' the man said, a look of disgust on his face. 'As in, Tommy Franks. Your number one tipper. Your biggest fan.'

Then it dawned on Dylan exactly who Tommy Franks was.

Yes, it was *definitely* him.

In his forties, bald and with a ratty mustache and soul patch combination.

That snarling, creepy voice.

It was Tommy Tipster. Real name, Tommy Franks.

Dylan immediately felt ill.

In his worst nightmares he hadn't imagined being kidnapped by one of his camming work customers.

This was like something out of a movie.

A horror movie at that.

'Tommy, please, let me go,' Dylan whimpered, struggling to hold back the tears. 'I... I don't deserve this.'

Dylan took an intake of shocked breath as he witnessed Tommy jump up and down on the spot. He was like a toddler having a tantrum.

'Don't deserve this? Don't deserve this?' Tommy screeched. 'But what about what *I* deserve?'

Dylan didn't know what to say.

Tommy seemed unhinged.

Dangerously so.

'I... don't... understand,' Dylan said, quietly, trying to stay calm.

'Well allow me to explain,' Tommy said, sneering as he prowled around Dylan. 'I spend all my money tipping you. Way more than any other cam-boy I watch. And what do I get in return? Nothing! You just stop camming without giving any explanation or notice. That's not right!'

Dylan didn't know how to respond.

He suddenly realized just how dangerous cam work could be for him and the other cam-boys. Sure, they were all adults, but there wasn't an instruction manual on how to deal with deranged customers. And there needed to be if Tommy was any indication of what could happen.

'Um–'

'Shut up!' Tommy said, cutting Dylan off before he could get a word out.

Tommy jumped up and down again, the soles of his shoes slapping hard against the concrete ground.

Dylan looked around again.

It appeared as if he was in a garage.

There was a beat-up old car in the corner. It looked seriously worse for wear, but Dylan wondered if it could possibly be used as some kind of getaway vehicle.

'I wouldn't bother trying to figure out a way out,' Tommy said, laughing maniacally. 'I've put some serious planning into this. You're mine now. There'll be no more walking out on me again. No fucking way.'

'Please, no. I'm begging you,' Dylan said, fighting back the tears. 'It doesn't have to be like this. There's always a way to change your life around. Trust me.'

Dylan was trying to help.

He could see that Tommy was a damaged individual.

If he could just make Tommy see sense, Dylan figured it was plausible that Tommy would let him walk.

But that was all well and true in theory.

In practice, it seemed much more unlikely.

Tommy didn't react well to Dylan's words.

Picking up an old pot of paint, Tommy threw it across the garage and up against the opposite wall.

The loud crashing noise made Dylan shake in fear.

But worse was to come...

'Hey, what's that red light?' Dylan said, trying to hide his nerves. 'The one there. The flashing red light?'

Tommy scurried around towards Dylan.

Dylan nearly threw up as he caught wind of Tommy's horribly stale odor. It was gross. Like Tommy hadn't bathed in weeks.

'That, my favorite cam buddy, is your camera!' Tommy said, a strong streak of menace in his voice. 'Smile, you're recording!'

Dylan felt his stomach twist and turn.

Tommy was recording him.

The whole situation had been recorded.

'You can't do this!' Dylan screamed. 'I have rights! Let me go! Release me now or I'm telling my Daddy!'

Tommy stopped in his tracks.

He was deadly still.

Totally silent.

'What did you just say?' Tommy said, his voice as cold as ice.

'I said I'm telling my Daddy on you!' Dylan said, repeating the words with extra emphasis this time. 'He'll find me, and he'll kick your mean butt all over this garage before taking you right down to the station.'

Tommy looked Dylan up and down.

He turned and made a big show of looking around the garage.

'Well unless he's a teeny-weenie little ant, I don't think I can see your so-called *Daddy* anywhere?' Tommy said, leering and taking pleasure in Dylan's distress. 'Ha! I'm always right. I knew you'd just be another loner cam worker. You've got no one. You made your Daddy up to try and scare me!'

Dylan shook his head.

He wanted to tell Tommy how wrong he was, but Dylan couldn't get any words out of his mouth.

'You're probably wondering why a handsome man like me loves cam workers so much?' Tommy said, chuckling away to himself as he played with his cell phone. 'Well, I'll tell you. I just love the control. I'm the one with the money. The other person is my servant. My slave. My employee. Worthless. Only there to do my bidding. It's hot.'

Dylan desperately wanted Flint to bang the door down and rescue him.

But how the hell would Flint even know where to look?

Yes, he was a detective, but Tommy was evidently very good at hiding his tracks.

Dylan decided that if he was going to get out of this mess, he would need to do some detective work himself. See if Tommy made any mistakes. Try and work some kind of angle to expose.

'Tommy, can I ask a question?' Dylan said, deliberately keeping his voice sounding as timid as possible. 'Please. Just one.'

Tommy seemed to get off from how shy and nervous Dylan seemed. He took a moment to think. Then grinned a horrible, smug smile.

'Shoot,' Tommy said. 'Ask away. I'm glad to see that you haven't totally lost your cam worker charms.'

'Thank you, Tommy,' Dylan said, hating himself for having to be so nice to this creep. 'How did you find me? You must be so clever. I could never think of how to do something like that.'

For a brief second it looked like Tommy knew what Dylan was up to. But his vanity and ego were obviously more important to him. Before Dylan knew it, Tommy was explaining in great detail what he had done.

'Well, it's pretty simple when you know what to do,' Tommy said. 'Especially if you have my set of skills. You see, I hacked your laptop. Not any old basic hack. Real deep hacking. The kind where I can access anything. And I mean *anything*. I've had a good old look at everything you have on that laptop. By the way, I'd suggest an upgrade. You could do with a new security package too. Ha!'

Tommy felt humiliated.

He was upset, scared, and totally freaked out by how devious Tommy was.

But he had to keep his mind on the mission.

He needed to keep Tommy talking.

Hopefully Tommy would slip up and reveal even the smallest detail that could help Dylan.

'Is that how you found out where I lived? By looking through my online accounts?' Dylan asked. 'I'm not very good with computers really. I wouldn't know where to begin.'

'No, an idiot little *cammer* like you wouldn't,' Tommy said dismissively as he cracked open a can of Sprite.

Tommy let out a long belching sound as he took a break from downing the Sprite.

It was disgusting.

Dylan couldn't help but make a face.

'Get used to it,' Tommy said. 'You're mine now. So, you'll have to deal with every inch of me. Including my love of fizzy drinks. Hey, if you perform well enough for me, I might even let you have the occasional can. But you need to *really* impress me for a treat like that. If you know what I mean.'

Dylan closed his eyes.

I wish-wish-wish-wish with all my heart.

Take me away from here.

Please-please-please-please rescue me...

But when Dylan opened his eyes, he was still locked up in the dark, damp garage. And Tommy was still there, taking photos of Dylan and generally being a leering, crazed slob.

'I realized I didn't answer your question,' Tommy laughed. 'I wouldn't want to deprive you of my wisdom. The answer is *yes,* I did find your location by looking through your laptop. It was a piece of cake.'

Dylan sighed.

If only he'd been with Flint for longer.

Flint would never have allowed something like this to happen.

No way.

'It could all have been so different,' Tommy continued. 'If you hadn't stopped camming, none of this would have been necessary. I could have carried on having my fun from a distance. But no. You had to stop. You had to try and be something else. But forget it. Once a cam-boy, always a cam-boy!'

Dylan cowered.

Things were going from bad to worse.

If anything, Tommy was getting more unhinged by the moment.

It was like he was running out of control the longer the situation went on. Tommy was obviously not stable in the first place, but now he had got what he wanted it was like he was going up another gear.

'Ha ha! And speaking of cam shows, now I get to have one any time I like,' Tommy cackled, totally out of control and almost bouncing around the garage. 'You'll do what I say. When I say. And how I say. No excuses. I'll have you doing the dirtiest, most explicit things imaginable. And I'll love every second of it. So will all the folks out there online as I broadcast it to the world!'

Dylan gulped.

He could feel himself sweating.

The garage was surprisingly cool given the heat outside, but that didn't stop Dylan's sweat.

This was like a waking nightmare.

Relentless.

Terrifying.

Dylan knew what he needed. Or rather *whom* he needed.

But Flint was nowhere to be seen. Yet.

All Dylan could do was pray that it wouldn't take long. He wasn't sure how much of Tommy he could handle. Tommy was gross. Totally yucky. Not the kind of person Dylan would ever want to spend time with – let alone be kidnapped by.

But this was the reality of the situation.

Dylan didn't even have Pinky with him to cuddle. That would have made things a little bit better.

But on the other hand, Dylan was actually glad that Pinky didn't have to be in this smelly old garage. Pinky deserved better.

Don't worry Pinky, we'll be back together soon.

Flint will save me.

Then the three of us can reunite forever.

'I need to do some stuff next door,' Tommy said. 'Behave. Don't even think about leaving. Oh, wait, you can't even if you wanted to! Anyway, have fun cam-boy and I'll see you soon.'

With that, Tommy hauled his ass out of the room.

Dylan was alone.

He was bound.

Trapped at Tommy's mercy.

Something had to give.

There had to be a way out.

There just *had* to be.

Chapter Eighteen

*Pull yourself together man. Call yourself a Daddy. Then act
like one damn it.*

Flint took a moment to steady himself.

He was spiraling.

The panic was well and truly setting in.

Flint's entire body felt heavy. Weak. The emotional toll
of what was happening was weighing on him. For all the
progress Flint had made recently, this was like a throwback
to the period after his partner Mickie had died.

Flint couldn't allow himself to wallow though.

He had to keep moving forward.

After discovering that Dylan was not at his apartment,
Flint had wondered momentarily if Dylan might have gone
back to his place.

There were other explanations for why the door had
been off its hinges.

Maintenance work.

The useless landlord quitting the job half-way through.

Even an attempted break in that got disturbed before it
got going.

Maybe these seemed like unlikely explanations, but they were possible in theory.

Flint knew from years of experience that it was foolish in the extreme to write off a twist or turn simply because it wasn't the most obvious option.

With that in mind, Flint had hot footed it back to his apartment. It was possible that Dylan had gone there.

There weren't any other realistic options that Dylan could choose.

Sure, maybe he could have gone to a café or bar, but not for this period of time. And not without taking his wallet that Flint had picked up on the table back at Dylan's place.

All bets were on Flint's home.

Flint *had* to believe that.

The alternative was just too terrifying.

But when Flint arrived at his place, he saw no sign of Dylan.

Worse than that though, there was not a single indication that Dylan had been there at any point in the day. Everything was untouched.

No, Flint's worst fears were coming true.

Dylan had gone.

It was at this point that Flint's mind began to fall back into old ways.

Negative thinking.

Pessimism.

The idea that he could never be a good Daddy.

That he just wasn't cut out to look after a Little.

Flint began to call Dylan's cell phone.

Over and over.

Each time it rang-out weighing heavier on Flint's heart.

Flint began to speculate. Rather than being kidnapped, was it possible that Dylan had simply run away from him?

After all, making him write those two hundred lines had been pretty harsh. It was the kind of punishment that didn't come with any kind of up-side. There was no sexy play after it. Only sore hands and two hundred repeated lines.

But if Dylan had hated it so much, why had he agreed in the first place?

And why had he even offered to repeat the whole thing after his solitary mistake?

Maybe Dylan had gone along with it simply to get Flint out of the apartment as quickly as possible. Then simply made his escape.

Flint had seen this kind of behavior before with his police work.

Runaways always tended to have a similar story once you got into it. And nine times out of ten it seemed to involve a breakdown in the home between the runaway and an overbearing or out of control authority figure.

Was that how Dylan might have viewed Flint?

'I'm such a fucking strict asshole,' Flint said, banging his fist on the kitchen table. 'Who the hell would want to be around me? It's no wonder he ran away. Fuck!'

Flint's head was spinning.

He didn't know which was more likely.

Whether Dylan had run away or been taken by someone else.

It was like his calm and rational detective brain had deserted him at precisely the worst moment.

Flint needed to focus.

Gather his thoughts and work out what the hell he should do.

Flint knew the police department was overworked in the extreme. Even calling in some favors he wouldn't be able to get this off the ground right away. Dylan was an adult after all. He wasn't obligated to tell Flint where he was. There was no way this would qualify as a missing person's case just yet.

Maybe the trouble with the stalker might mean Flint could leverage some earlier than usual investigations. But even that was nowhere near enough. Not even close.

Flint didn't have time to wait.

And neither did Dylan.

Flint decided to contact Dylan again.

But this time he would send a message rather than call.

Dylan. It's me, Flint. Daddy. I'm sorry about making you do those lines. If you don't ever want to see me again, it's fine. I get it. Honestly, I do. I just need to know you're safe. That's all. Please. Flint.

Flint put the phone down on the kitchen worktop and decided to take a closer look around the apartment. He hadn't checked the bedroom yet, there could be a clue in there.

Even the slightest hint as to where Dylan might have gone would be a bonus.

As Flint inspected the bedroom, he looked over at the scattered array of toys and stuffies that he had bought for Dylan.

Flint was a tough man.

Hard as nails.

But in this moment, he felt a surge of raw emotion.

His Little was missing. Possibly in danger.

Flint felt like crap.

He needed to be out there, searching for Dylan.

Trying every possible angle he could think of.

There had to be something he was missing. Somewhere. Even the smallest detail.

Flint moved on from the bedroom and had a look in the bathroom. All of Dylan's toiletries were still there. It felt unlikely to Flint that Dylan would have run away without his treasured Disney electric toothbrush. That didn't make sense at all. Dylan loved it so much, even joking to Flint that he would buy him a special Daddy Disney electric toothbrush for Christmas.

No, the more Flint thought about it, the less likely it seemed that Dylan had simply run away from him. Flint couldn't rule it out altogether, but it just didn't add up.

There was definitely something sinister afoot.

Flint felt his mind begin to focus.

It was a similar feeling to the one he experienced back in his early years.

Instinct.

Burning desire.

A laser-focus on detail.

Flint ran back into the living area and ran his hands up and down surfaces. He buried his fingers in between the plumped cushions on the couch.

Searching.

Hoping.

At that moment, even the smallest, slightest detail could help.

Flint had solved some big cases with the smallest nuances. It could be done. It was often how the best police work was completed. Going all the way back to his first day in the academy, Flint had been earmarked as having the potential to rise all the way to the top.

He could think outside of the box.

He was meticulous too.

What Flint needed now was a return to those days.

It wasn't the time to overthink things, but Flint wished he hadn't let his career fall into a rut.

Had he kept on progressing, things might be so different.

He would be a different person.

He would have known how better to deal with Dylan.

And as a result, Dylan would be safe right now.

Suddenly, Flint heard his phone ping.

'Oh shit, it's Dylan,' Flint said as he scrabbled across the room and into the kitchen.

But no sooner than Flint had picked up his phone, his face turned to grey.

Flint was aghast.

Shocked.

He couldn't believe what he was reading.

It was like each and every one of his worst nightmares was coming true all in one disgustingly flippant text message...

You are never going to see Dylan again, 'Daddy'. EVER. He belongs to ME now. Not you. But ME.

Flint felt his legs go weak.

It was like the usual power that fueled his huge, muscular legs had suddenly been turned off at the mains supply.

'What... have... I... done...,' Flint said, burying his face in his palms as he took a seat. 'This can't be happening. Can it?'

Flint didn't know what to do.

He was in a state of total shock and time was very much against him. He had to do something. There had to be some kind of shortcut.

There was no way of knowing who sent that message.

It was clearly the same person who had been stalking Dylan. That much was obvious. But beyond that, Flint was drawing major blanks.

This was a worst nightmare type of scenario for a cop.

Made a million times worse by Flint's personal connection to Dylan.

It was a time sensitive situation with no obvious game plan.

But defeat was not an option.

There was no way Flint was going to quit.

It wasn't all bad.

Firstly, Flint knew that Dylan was alive.

That was one thing.

The second thing was that the person who was holding Dylan was open to communication.

This could lead to a mistake, or a clue being revealed.

But Flint knew that the online world wasn't exactly in his wheelhouse.

He needed help.

Suddenly, it became clear.

It was obvious in fact.

Without a moment's hesitation, Flint picked up his cellphone and dialed a number.

'It's me,' Flint said. 'I need your help. Serious emergency. It's time to see if we really are Hero Daddies or not.'

Chapter Nineteen

Okay, don't panic.

Think about what Flint would do.

He's not here, but he could still help...

Dylan began to breath slowly. In and out. Over and over.

Gradually his heart rate returned to something approaching normal. Dylan felt his mind clearing up a little. No more tears fell. His lip stopped trembling.

It was time to work out how he was going to get out of here.

Dylan had worked too hard in his life recently to end up as some tied-up cam-boy.

He had a romance novel to record and a Daddy to hug.

'Okay, okay, I think these bindings might not be as tight as I thought,' Dylan whispered.

Saying the words out loud made him feel more confident.

It was a trick that Flint had taught him.

Verbalizing what you wanted was a great way of making

it happen. Sure, it was a slightly corny Daddy saying, but there was undoubtedly a whole heap of truth to it.

Dylan began to slowly work up some steam as he rubbed and pulled, his wrists slowly beginning to loosen at the back of the chair.

What he really needed to do was get them completely free from the chair legs. If he could just manage that, then he would be halfway there.

Not all the way.

But some of the way to freedom at least.

There was a loud clattering noise coming from beyond the door that Tommy had exited.

Dylan froze.

'Do not come back in here. Repeat do not come back in here,' Dylan whispered.

It was an agonizing wait.

If Tommy came back and suspected that Dylan had been trying to escape, he would freak out. Probably tie Dylan even tighter.

Or worse.

He might do something more extreme.

Dylan didn't even want to consider what Tommy might do.

It wasn't worth it.

Wasted energy.

Dylan waited a few moments longer and began to struggle and pull at his ties even harder.

He was making progress.

It wasn't fast, and it hurt his wrists, but he could feel the ties moving and slackening.

As Dylan continued to attempt to free himself, he cast his mind back to Flint. It was impossible not to. Flint had been such a huge inspiration in his life pretty much from the moment they met.

The connection between them was the real deal.

If Dylan hadn't already realized it, he did now.

Maybe it was the drama of the situation he found himself in, but he knew from the bottom of his heart that Flint was his Forever Daddy.

Speaking of peril, Dylan shook his wrists so hard that the entire chair toppled over, taking Dylan with it.

Fortunately, Dylan was able to stop his head smacking against the cold concrete floor. That was a potential disaster averted.

But what was he going to do now?

With one hard pull, Dylan freed his arms.

His wrists were still tied together with super-sticky tape, but he was only a meter or so away from the old car.

'Come on, think,' Dylan whispered, his breathing heavy after the fall. 'I've got a Daddy and a stuffie to get home to.'

Dylan began to crawl over towards the car.

It wasn't easy.

The floor was rough underneath him and Dylan could feel the friction grazing his skin. But he was determined to do this. There was no way he was going to give up and accept his fate as Tommy's personal cam-boy.

No way.

Dylan was at the beginning of building a life for himself. There were too many good times ahead for him to give in and let someone else take that all away from him.

As he inched closer to the car, he spotted the exact point he would use to try and cute the rope around his wrists. The car's exhaust was pretty much totally broken.

It was rusty.

Hanging half off the car.

But it had sharp edges.

Exactly the kind of edges that could cut through the rope.

'Okay, let's do this,' Dylan said, a determined steel in his voice that if it was an octave or two lower could have come out of Flint's mouth. 'Work methodically. Slowly but surely. I can do this!'

With that, Dylan got himself in position and began to rub his wrists up and down against the exhaust pipe.

It was risky.

If Dylan rubbed too hard or if he missed the rope, he could end up cutting himself badly. And given how rusty the exhaust pipe was, that could have incredibly dangerous consequences.

As much as Dylan wanted to escape, he had to pace himself.

Slow and steady.

One wrong move and there could be trouble.

'Nearly there, keep going,' Dylan whispered, still conscious that Tommy could walk in at any time.

Dylan couldn't spend any time worrying about the consequences of Tommy discovering him though. It was now or never. Dylan simply had to press ahead and keep on going.

In fact, the whole situation kind of reminded him of his breakup with his old Daddy. The one who treated him terribly.

When Dylan had realized that he had to get out of that relationship, he felt scared. Afraid of how his ex would react to Dylan saying he wanted to leave. It really hadn't been a very good relationship at all.

And Dylan even postponed leaving his former Daddy

he was so afraid of what might happen. Over and over. Each time he backed out of leaving, Dylan just felt worse.

That was until one final day where his Daddy shared video footage of Dylan with some of his other friends. It was the kind of X-Rated footage that really should stay between couples, unless otherwise agreed of course.

Dylan felt heartbroken.

It had been so painful to experience.

But it gave him the final push he needed to leave.

And that was it. He had waited until his Daddy had gone to work and then simply packed up his stuff and left. Without saying a word. Without wasting a single moment. He knew he had to get out of the apartment and never look back.

In some ways it was the hardest step he had ever taken.

But in other ways, it was the easiest.

And now, lying on the floor and desperately trying to cut his ties, Dylan knew he had one option and one option only.

It was time to get out and never look back.

'Just... one... more... yay!' Dylan said, letting out a tiny whoop of joy as he managed to free his hands.

Success!

Dylan quickly got onto his knees and using his now free hands set about untying his feet. Tommy had used extra-sticky tape on top of the rope, so it was taking time.

More time than Dylan wanted to spend.

But he had no choice.

Dylan was now frantically pulling and tearing the tape to get down to the rope.

'Nearly there, come on,' Dylan said, his heart rate increasing the closer he got to finally freeing himself.

Dylan didn't exactly know what he would do once he

was freed from the ropes. He cast his eyes around the garage and wondered whether he would be able to pull up the main garage door.

It should be possible.

Dylan certainly didn't want to go inside the building and risk crossing paths with Tommy.

That would be absolutely the last resort.

Ideally, Dylan would be able to locate the opening mechanism for the garage door and escape out on to the street that way. Dylan figured that there was no way Tommy would try and take him back once Dylan was out on the street.

There would surely be people around.

And for a coward and creep like Tommy, that meant it was a no-go zone. Twisted individuals like Tommy were bullies. The second that they had to do anything in public they usually retreated into their shells.

Even if he tries to grab me on the street, I'll scream.

Louder than the loudest unicorn who's just stepped on a sharp shell.

Come on... nearly-nearly-nearly there...

Suddenly, the rope binds snapped in two and Dylan was free and able to continue on his mission to get out of Tommy's garage.

Or at least he thought he was.

Dylan heard a click.

He froze.

Then turning his head slightly, he looked up and saw Tommy standing over him. Pointing a gun directly at his head.

Dylan was terrified.

His attempted escape had all been for nothing.

And now things looked a whole lot worse.

'Where do you think you're going, cam-boy?' Tommy said, a sly smile on his face. He was enjoying tormenting Dylan.

Dylan was speechless.

The sight of Tommy holding the cocked and loaded gun was too much. Things were even worse than Dylan had feared.

Not only was Tommy unhinged, but he was extremely dangerous too.

'I said, where do you think you're going?' Tommy repeated, a menacing tone to his voice. 'Answer me!'

Dylan stuttered and stammered but couldn't get a single word out of his mouth.

He was panicking.

In a state of total shock.

This nightmare had just got a hundred times worse.

With his escape attempt now officially dead in the water, Dylan had no option but to do exactly as Tommy desired.

There was no telling how far Tommy would push things. If Dylan had learned one thing about Tommy Franks, it was that he had no concept of boundaries. Of what society deemed as acceptable behavior.

Tommy was operating outside of the law and seemingly had no intention of doing the right thing and letting Dylan walk free.

Dylan's one remaining hope was that Flint would somehow work out where he was and come to his rescue. But even then, Flint would have no idea that Tommy had a gun.

Things could get explosive.

Dylan said a silent prayer.

He needed his Daddy, and he needed him right that second.

Chapter Twenty

Jackson was due to arrive at Flint's apartment at any moment.

The wait was agonizing.

Flint had called Jackson because he figured with Jackson's hacking abilities, he may well be able to somehow locate Dylan.

It was a long shot, but one that Flint just had to try.

'Come on, Jackson!' Flint said, the frustration flowing out of his mouth as he paced around the kitchen, desperate to get this seek and rescue mission up and running.

As a firefighter, Jackson was no stranger to moving quickly.

Part of his job was based on making quick, confident decisions under pressure. Flint figured that even if Jackson couldn't help locate Dylan, he would definitely bring some added intelligence to the situation.

Jackson's problem-solving skills were legendary.

He had been awarded several medals by the city for bravery. But he wasn't the type of firefighter to rush in and go gung-ho. No, he was calm, methodical, and able to make clear-headed assessments at rapid speed.

Flint would have called his other Daddy friend, Luther. He too as an ER doctor had the kind of mental and physical skill set that would have come in extremely handy. The only problem was that Dom was on a night shift at the ER.

This meant one thing... no cell phone access.

Oh, and the likelihood that Luther had about a hundred cases of injured people to deal with and not much time to do it in.

Hopefully, Jackson would be enough.

That was what Flint was banking on anyway.

Just as he was about to get concerned as to Jackson's whereabouts, there was an urgent knocking at Flint's door.

'Jackson!' Flint said, the relief in his voice very apparent.

'My bro, I came as fast as I could,' Jackson said, the pair embracing in what was an epic display of two big Daddies showing their love for each other.

Two large, protective men.

Each with a dominant side.

Physically capable of meeting any challenge.

And crucially, working on the same side to find Dylan.

'What's that?' Flint said as he witnessed Jackson take a seat at the kitchen table and unpack his backpack to reveal two laptops, a couple of small black boxes, and a whole bunch of wires. 'Actually, don't bother. Just get to work.'

'On it,' Jackson said, his warm brown eyes fixated on the dual screens. 'Okay. Okay. This shouldn't take too long. Any chance of an espresso?'

Flint rolled his eyes and then nodded.

Jackson loved coffee.

Maybe it was a firefighter thing. Or it could have been a

hacker trait. Either way, when there was work to be done, Jackson always worked best with a caffeine injection.

The stronger the better.

'Here's a triple shot,' Flint said, placing an espresso cup down next to Jackson as he tapped on the keys with serious intent. 'I can't even imagine doing what you do. It's like another language to me.'

'Maybe because it literally is another language?' Jackson laughed, downing his triple espresso in one hearty gulp. 'Never mind. Now step back and watch the master at work.'

Jackson began to work in a frenzied overdrive.

It was spectacular to witness.

Flint could do nothing but watch. His input wasn't needed. But what exactly was Jackson doing?

'Okay, *neeeeearly* there,' Jackson grinned, his dimples almost glowing with pride. 'Any moment now I should have hacked into the laptop and.... *Bam!* We're in!'

Flint punched the air in excitement.

After a quick high-five, Jackson continued to work his magic.

'Location?' Flint said, his voice full of anticipation. 'We need a location.'

'Got it, let's go,' Jackson said.

Without further ado, the two Daddies stormed out of Flint's place and made their way outside.

'Let's ride,' Jackson said, pointing over at his Harley. 'Come on. I know a shortcut that involves some seriously nimble riding.'

'So what are you saying?' Flint replied, jumping on the back of the super-charged motorcycle.

'I'm saying, hang the fuck on,' Jackson laughed. 'Things are about to get wild.'

* * *

Jackson wasn't lying when he told Flint to hang on tight.

The ride over to the location was intense.

As part of Jackson's training as a firefighter he had been on several extreme-driving courses. Three involved cars and firetrucks, but there was also an option to take the motorcycle unit too.

Jackson had been more than happy to take this option up.

Flint felt momentarily queasy as he got off the bike.

One too many near-misses along the way that probably aged Flint at least ten years.

But that wasn't important.

Nothing in that moment was more important than finding Dylan and dealing with whichever scumbag had taken him.

'Okay, this is the place,' Jackson said. 'What do you think? Storm in? Stealth?'

Flint took a moment to observe the building.

Yes, time was of the essence. But on the other hand, now they were here they needed to make a calm and considered assessment. There was no point having gone to the effort of finding out the location only to blow it all by making the wrong move.

It was an old, grimy looking building.

The front door to the side looked like it was about to fall off.

The wooden windows looked chipped, like they were deep into the process of rotting away. The drapes were dirty and mangled, barely hanging on to the rail.

Flint shuddered at the thought of Dylan being held captive in there. It was no way for his Little to live. And if

Flint had anything to do with it, today would be the last time that Dylan ever had to see this damned hell hole.

'That garage door,' Flint said. 'A million bucks and a whole load of police experience tells me that we can jimmy that open quick and easy.'

Jackson nodded.

'Concur totally,' Jackson said, his muscular arms flexing as they poked out from outside of his trademarked brilliant-white t-shirt. 'Let's do this thing.'

Flint was about to open the garage door when he heard a slight noise from inside.

'There's someone in the garage,' Flint whispered. 'Sounds like there could be two people in there. Change of plan. Follow my lead.'

Flint decided that a surprise entrance was a bad idea.

He had no idea of what was going on inside, so couldn't take the chance on a sudden entrance. Flint didn't know who he was dealing with, or what they were capable of.

It just wasn't worth risking any unnecessary harm to his beloved Dylan.

Flint took a deep breath and knocked on the small door to the side of the main garage door.

'It's the police,' Flint said, his voice loud and author-itative.

Jackson and Flint exchanged glances as they waited for a response. Any kind of response. There was definitely someone in there, so the fact they weren't answering wasn't likely to be good news.

'Repeat. This is the police. Open the door right now,' Flint said, his voice louder, more intimidating. 'I will not ask again.'

Still no response.

Flint could hear some rummaging around going on inside.

Whoever was in there could definitely hear him.

The time for talking was over.

It was time for action.

After counting to three, both Flint and Jackson smashed down the smaller door. It was old, rotten, just like the rest of the building. It caved easily.

Flint's eyes were immediately drawn across the small, damp room.

'Dylan!'

'Flint!' Dylan cried, his voice full of fear.

It was Flint's worst nightmare.

He was confronted by the sight of Dylan being held at gunpoint.

'Don't move a *freakin'* muscle,' Tommy said, holding Dylan right up against his body. 'One wrong move and your so-called Little gets it.'

Flint exchanged a quick look with Jackson.

It was a time for cool heads.

Sure, they could easily overpower Dylan's captor, but there was no way in hell they were risking Dylan being hurt in the process.

'Okay, okay, it's all good,' Jackson said, calming stepping back and keeping his hands visible. 'My man, why not let Flint here talk to you. Real relaxed. No stress.'

Flint nodded.

He knew that this was a pivotal moment.

'Don't try and talk to me, cop,' Tommy said, sounding like he was frothing at the mouth. 'I'm the one in charge here. I'm in control. Dylan is mine!'

Flint had dealt with people like Tommy before.

He was obviously disenchanted with the world. Sad. A

loner. And now this was his attempt at regaining some control. An attempt to make his existence at least a little bit better.

But Tommy had to be stopped.

Tommy's life may well have sucked, but Flint knew that this was no excuse.

It was time to apply some pressure.

'Okay, you're in control,' Flint said, taking tiny steps forward. 'Everyone here agrees, right?'

'Y-y-y-yes, Tommy is in control,' Dylan said, two large tears falling down his cheek.

'For sure, the main man Tommy is on top,' Jackson said, smiling and showing off those incredible dimples. 'Nice car by the way. I love a good project. This could be super nice if you cleaned it up.'

Tommy seemed to relax a little bit.

The tension in the room was still palpable, but the heat had perhaps come down a few degrees.

There was still work to do.

'Tommy, it's okay, there's no drama here,' Flint said, continuing to edge forward ever so slightly. 'This doesn't have to be a big deal. No big deal *at all*. We're all good. Right?'

Tommy looked like he was having a moment of doubt.

He still had the gun pointed at Dylan, but Flint could see that Tommy's grip was looser. Like he was shying away from the prospect of firing the gun.

This was good.

This was progress.

'Tell me, Tommy,' Flint said. 'Do you like to read? I find it very relaxing. I recently discovered audiobooks too. Right, Dylan?'

Dylan nodded, nervous but looking as if he was clued

up to Flint's tactics. This was about talking Tommy down from the ledge, not smashing him off it.

'You can't beat a nice bit of steamy romance while reading in a hot bubble bath,' Flint continued. 'Hot water. Relaxing bubbles. Maybe a candle. Some light music in the background...'

It appeared as if Flint's words were taking Tommy on a journey.

Flint saw Tommy lower his gun away from Dylan for a moment.

This was Flint's chance, he had to go for it.

It was now or never.

Jumping forwards, Flint crashed into Tommy and quickly wrestled him to the ground.

'*Aargh*! You tricked me! You asshole!' Tommy cried out, pure rage in his voice.

Jackson quickly moved over and helped Flint restrain Tommy.

'No sudden moves, Tommy,' Flint said. 'We don't want to hurt you. But understand me when I say this... it's all over. You're done here.'

'I've got him from here,' Jackson said, holding Tommy down with ease. 'You go to Dylan. It looks like he needs his Daddy.'

Flint nodded and immediately ran over to Dylan.

'Daddy, you kept me safe!' Dylan said, burying his face deep into Flint's chest. 'I always knew you'd come. I always believed. I was so scared though.'

'It looks like you were being very brave to me,' Flint said, gripping Dylan in an extra cozy Daddy bear hug. 'You're the bravest Little in the whole of New York City.'

Dylan smiled and hugged Flint even harder.

'But what about Tommy?' Dylan said. 'It was him all

along. The photos and everything. I hate him. He nearly ruined everything for us.'

Flint looked over towards Tommy. Jackson was still holding him down. The police were on their way now and it wouldn't be long before they arrived.

'You don't ever need to worry about him again,' Flint said. 'Tommy will be going away for a long time. Seriously long in fact. Hopefully he'll put his time to good use and learn right from wrong. But that's his problem to work out, not yours.'

Dylan and Flint embraced again.

Flint bowed his head and planted a big kiss on Dylan's forehead.

It felt good.

They had worked together, Tommy was going down, and the path was clear for them to enjoy being Daddy and Little again.

Everything was good in the world.

And things were about to get even better too.

Chapter Twenty-One

After being rescued by Flint and Jackson, the next few weeks for Dylan were all about getting his life back to normality.

It wasn't easy at first.

Getting over something like being kidnapped never would be.

But that being said, it wasn't too long before Dylan was enjoying life again.

Dylan was determined to live life to the fullest.

Both in terms of his new career as a voice artist and also his social life too.

Dylan and Flint had begun going out together as Daddy and Little. It was a good feeling.

They had *nothing* to be ashamed of.

It was so freeing to know that they had got over what was surely the toughest opening to a relationship imaginable. And come out the other side of things feeling more in love than ever too.

From now on, even the sternest challenge would be a walk in the park.

Dylan had moved in with Flint.

He didn't feel any regrets about leaving his old apartment. Too many bad memories. Oh, and the world's worst aircon system too.

Flint had made plenty of allowances to make his apartment more Little-friendly.

The guest room had been converted into Dylan's own playroom. It was no longer the neutral, minimalist guest room of old. Instead, it was all about color, joy, and just about an endless supply of toys and coloring equipment.

Dylan knew he was a lucky Little.

Flint was a keeper, that was for sure.

But it wasn't just at home that the good times were happening.

Dylan and Flint had started hanging out at The Little Club. It was one of a growing number of venues that catered specifically to Daddies and Littles.

Plus their kinks too.

Before long, both Dylan and Flint had made plenty of new Daddy and Little friends. They were non-judgmental, kind and totally welcoming.

Exactly the kind of people that it felt good to be around.

Dylan rarely thought of Tommy anymore. As the ordeal faded into the back of his mind, Dylan even took the opportunity to talk to the counselor at the Little Club. The counsellor helped Dylan learn techniques and process the trauma in a way that would give him long-term closure.

Sometimes Dylan wouldn't feel like going to a session, but he always had Flint there to warn him what happened to Littles who didn't stick to their schedules.

And here's a clue – it involved a paddle!

'Hey, Dylan, shall I get you a fresh juice box?' Flint

said, hollering over from the Little Club bar where he was enjoying a beer with some fellow Daddies.

'Yes please, Daddy!' Dylan called back, a broad grin on his face as he watched his hunky Daddy speak to the server.

Dylan was hanging out with Casper.

It was good to have this kind of normality back in his life.

And it was also so good to no longer have any need to do the cam work.

'It just wasn't me,' Dylan said, thinking back to his time as a cam-boy. 'I'd never judge anyone for doing it though. It's about whatever feels good for you, right?'

Casper agreed.

Flicking his peroxide fringe back to one side, Casper finished off his own juice. His bright blue eyes were full of sparkle.

Dylan sensed that Casper had a Daddy on his mind.

But *who*?

Casper had been single for a long time.

He was busy with his career and that made dating hard at times.

'Okay, so you've definitely got a crush on one of the Daddies here!' Dylan squealed, his voice full of excitement. 'Tell me! I promise I won't tell anyone. Not even Flint.'

Casper had a doubtful look in his eye.

'There's no way you can keep a secret from Flint,' Casper said. 'I know for a fact he's got way more than one way to get you to confess!'

The two Littles laughed.

They both knew exactly what Casper was referring too.

Dylan even went a little red as he thought back to all the amazing sex that he and Flint had been having recently. Dylan was getting better and better at the whole orgasm control thing. It was no wonder, Flint was a superb teacher in that respect.

'Well, okay, I'll tell y–'

But before Casper could dish the details, both Flint and Jackson arrived back at the table.

Flint handed Dylan his juice box and had come with one for Casper too.

'Thank you, Daddy,' Dylan said, a look of pure love aimed in Flint's direction.

'Thank you, Flint,' Casper said, eagerly piercing the lid of the juice box and beginning to suck it down.

'Hey, slow down young dude,' Jackson said, placing his hand briefly on Casper's shoulder.

Casper immediately went bright red.

He had perfectly porcelain skin, so the second he blushed the whole world knew about it.

Dylan watched as Casper quickly composed himself and carried on drinking.

This was interesting.

Was Jackson the Daddy that Casper was crushing on?

But Dylan didn't have too long to wonder.

Jackson and Flint began to recall the day that they saved Dylan. It was a wonderful story. Listening to it being told by the two Daddies was almost as good as listening to an action-adventure audiobook before bedtime.

Dylan and Flint were holding hands underneath the table. As fun as it undoubtedly was to be out with their friends, their focus was always on each other.

It was a physical connection, but so much more at the same time. It was feeling a lot like love.

'I bet you've got even more stories from your life as a firefighter,' Casper said, making sure to make eye contact with Jackson. 'What's it like sliding down that pole so often?'

Dylan, Casper and the other Littles who were now in attendance all started to giggle.

The Daddies simply rolled their eyes and chuckled.

'Maybe you'll find out one day,' Jackson said, stretching his powerful arms up in the air to reveal a couple of super-hot tattoos on his defined inner arms. 'But what happens at the station, stays at the station. Got it?'

The heat was definitely building between Casper and Jackson.

So much so that Jackson got up to go and dance, taking Dylan and the rest of the Littles with him.

'Do not say a *word!*' Casper said, shouting over the music as the resident DJ Little Damian played another pop-tastic hit. 'It was just harmless banter. We're friends. It could never go any further. We're both too busy.'

'*Hmmm,* if you say so,' Dylan said, dancing and jumping with Casper as the music raged on. 'I'll believe you but a squillion-million others wouldn't!'

The Littles all laughed.

It was fun when a potential Daddy and Little romance was brewing. But Casper and Jackson's story would have to wait for another time. Right at that moment it was purely about having fun together on the dance floor.

They were ready to dance the night away!

* * *

Dylan and Flint actually decided to call it a night fairly early.

They both had a lot on at that moment with work and decided to be strict with their bedtimes. Flint had allowed for one or possibly two late nights per week, and the pair of them wanted to save their late nights for the weekend.

That kind of made the best sense.

There was a big party at the Little Club on Saturday night that the pair of them were looking forward to.

For Dylan that meant lots and lots of playing and dancing.

For Flint, it was a nice and relaxed evening in the company of lots of like-minded Daddies. Each one with their own story to tell.

Dylan and Flint arrived back at their place in good spirits.

But the evening wasn't quite over yet.

There was one more activity that Dylan had actually been dreading.

It was a trust exercise.

One that the counsellor at the Little Club had suggested for Dylan. It required him to be blindfolded and fall backwards into Flint's arms.

Dylan had been dreading it.

It wasn't that he didn't trust Flint's strength.

Far from it, Flint was one of the strongest Daddies there was. Strong, flexible, and with great hand-eye coordination. From a physical point of view, Dylan knew he had virtually nothing to fear.

But of course, it wasn't about that.

Trust was emotional.

And given his experiences with his former Daddy and then more recently with what happened with the stalker Tommy Franks, Dylan knew he still had to take a final step when it came to trust.

It was a big deal for him.

Flint knew that too.

That was why Flint had up to this point not pushed it too hard. Dylan appreciated that greatly. It showed how patient and caring a Daddy Flint was.

But time was ticking.

The exercise needed to be completed before Dylan's next counselling session.

'Dylan, I think we need to... you know,' Flint said, standing in nothing but his pajama bottoms as he emerged from the bedroom.

'You mean... the falling backwards thing, don't you?' Dylan said, himself only wearing his tiny little Calvin Klein briefs. 'I'm still a bit scared. But...'

With that, Dylan decided that it was in fact time he took the next step. He stood in front of Flint and took a moment to prepare himself.

All the while, Flint stood patiently behind him.

Dylan could sense that Flint was there.

It felt less terrifying than Dylan had imagined it would.

But he'd never know unless he actually took the step and allowed himself to fall backwards.

Dylan took a big breath, inhaled, and let it happen.

He fell backwards.

As Dylan fell, everything seemed to move in slow motion.

His mind was at once both totally clear and also full of memories. His life had changed so much since he met Flint. Sure, it had happened in a bad moment in Dylan's life, but that wasn't important any longer.

Dylan was happy now.

He was a Little with his Forever Daddy.

Dylan was more confident, focused, and had a great new career building. He was creative every day. He had voiceover work offers filling up his inbox.

In fact, things had been going so well with the voice acting that Dylan had even been approached by a talent agent who was well known in the industry for working with Littles and giving them a safe and specialized environment to succeed in.

Dylan knew he was lucky.

Everything had fallen perfectly into place.

Speaking of falling...

'Hey, you did it!' Flint said, gently catching Dylan in his arms before bringing him in for a big cuddle. 'That's another goal you can put down as well and truly completed.'

Dylan had learned to trust again.

He'd learned how to love.

And found the perfect Daddy to do it with.

Dylan and Flint kissed.

It was the perfect moment, one that Dylan would never, *ever* forget.

Chapter Twenty-Two

Flint was full of pride to see Dylan finally get over his fear and complete the falling backward task.

It felt like one final step had been completed.

Flint couldn't believe how far the pair of them had come. Both as individuals and as a couple.

They were now a Daddy and Little.

A team.

The *perfect* combination.

Flint would sometimes look back on his life and wonder if all of the pain he had suffered via the death of his former partner and the years that followed was somehow part of a larger plan.

A plan that was always going to lead him to Dylan.

Flint wasn't much of a philosopher in truth.

But he thought back to the very first time he caught sight of Dylan at the police station.

Flint had never seen anyone cuter.

Even in a distressed state, Flint could see how beautiful Dylan was. It was like he was the perfect version of a Little.

Flint's dick certainly felt that way, that was for sure.

With Dylan's forever spankable butt in nothing but a pair of small white briefs that evening, Flint couldn't resist reaching around and giving each cheek a good squeeze.

'Daddy! That's naughty!' Dylan said, a twinkle in his eye.

Flint grunted.

His Daddy Dom instinct was kicking in.

And judging by the way his dick was growing inside his pajama bottoms, it was coming on strong too.

Flint picked Dylan up and carried him into the bedroom.

The heatwave was finally breaking outside.

In fact, the rain was pouring down and rattling the windows.

It created a tender, romantic vibe in their bedroom.

Flint lay Dylan down on the bed and began by kissing over Dylan's smooth, pale chest.

'That feels so good,' Dylan purred, his body reacting to every single touch from Flint. 'I don't know how long I'll last tonight.'

Flint laughed.

He had been training Dylan using his orgasm control and denial methods. Usually there was a large dose of punishment and pain to go alongside those, but tonight it was all about pleasure.

That didn't mean that Flint would allow Dylan to cum any time soon, however. He wanted to prolong the pleasure for as long as was humanly possible.

'I'm going to kiss every inch of your body,' Flint said, his gravelly voice sending vibrations all over Dylan. 'I'll keep you just on the edge. Over and over. When the time comes, it will be the best orgasm of your life.'

Dylan's faced flushed red.

185

Flint knew how much Dylan enjoyed his dirty talk.

Flint proceeded to slowly pull Dylan's Calvin Klein's down and watched with animal lust as Dylan's hard dick sprung out.

'Looks like I'll have my work cut out stopping you from blowing,' Flint chuckled, giving Dylan's cock a firm squeeze.

Flint got naked too and the pair of them began to intertwine their bodies, rolling around on the bed as they kissed each other passionately.

There was a total freedom in how they expressed themselves.

They felt utterly comfortable in one another's company.

Flint smiled as Dylan wrapped his hands around Flint's rock-hard cock and began to jerk it.

'That's good, but let's add some lube,' Flint said, reaching over to his bedside cupboard and taking out a fresh pot of lubricant. 'You put it on mine, I'll work some onto yours.'

Dylan followed Flint's instructions and they each began to massage the sticky, wet lube onto their partner's dick.

'Is this a new lube? It's super-extra-tingly!' Dylan said, moaning as Flint began to jerk him quicker. 'It feels... *amazing.*'

Flint smiled.

It was indeed a new lube, one that came highly recommended from Kieran, the man who ran the sex shop. Kieran was a Daddy too, so knew exactly what Littles liked to feel on their dicks.

'Yeah, and speaking of something new,' Flint said, a glint in his eye. 'I picked this up a few weeks ago. I guess with you so close to cumming, now is the perfect time to try it.'

Dylan's eyes lit up as Flint reached under the bed and lifted his hand to reveal he was holding a brand-new paddle. It was the one that Flint had purchased on the day that Dylan had been taken by Tommy Franks.

It hadn't seemed right to use it before.

But now felt like a good time.

'Now turn around and show me that cute little butt,' Flint said. 'I'm going to give you a few hard, fast swats. Nothing major. Just enough to keep your excitement under control.'

Dylan yelped with joy as Flint did as he promised. His spanks were as accurate and consistently stingy as always.

'That's enough for now,' Flint said, his breathing a little heavier as he took in the gorgeous sight of Dylan's glowing ass cheeks. 'Let me rub some lotion onto that tushy for you.'

Flint picked Dylan up and lay him across his lap.

It was a pleasure to apply the lotion and slowly massage it into Dylan's soft, peachy ass.

Dylan enjoyed it too. It wasn't long before Flint could feel Dylan's dick stiffening again and pressing up against his rock-hard thigh.

'Do I need to paddle you some more, or can you control yourself?' Flint said, gently reaching down and running his hands over Dylan's cock.

'I'm good... I think!' Dylan giggled.

'*Hmm*, you need something to do to keep your mind occupied,' Flint said. 'Get on your knees and show me how well you can suck cock.'

Dylan didn't hesitate.

He sprung up from Flint's lap and immediately positioned himself so that he could grip Flint's dick in both hands and begin working his plump lips over Flint's swollen dick head.

It made Flint truly horny to see how responsive Dylan was to his commands. The dynamic between them was ideal. Just perfect in fact.

Dylan was sucking and bobbing his head all the way down to the base of Flint's shaft. It felt so good. For a moment, it was Flint who had to worry about cumming too soon.

'Okay, that's enough young man,' Flint bellowed, lifting Dylan up off his dick and drawing him back down onto the bed with him.

Flint and Dylan resumed rolling around together, Flint's big leg resting on top of Dylan's body. Pinning his Little in position. Securing *total* control.

'I feel so safe with you,' Dylan said, his pupils dilated as the sexual energy rose and rose. 'I want to do something for you. Anything. You name it.'

Flint smiled.

'Maybe it's time I do something for you,' Flint replied, a look of pure desire in his face.

Flint proceeded to flip Dylan over onto his front.

His large hands parted Dylan's ass cheeks and Flint began to lick and swirl his tongue over Dylan's tight hole.

Dylan whimpered in pleasure.

The more Flint worked his tongue, the louder and more ecstatic Dylan's gasps of pleasure became.

Flint wasn't sure how long he could keep Dylan from shooting his load. It felt like one more touch or lick would send him beyond the point of no return.

It was time for something else.

With Dylan's hole already wet from Flint's tongue, Flint added a little bit of lube and gently worked it inside Dylan's ass.

Dylan instinctively lifted his hips and presented his ass in the perfect position for Flint.

'Take me, fill me up and have the best orgasm you can,' Dylan said. 'I'll wait for mine.'

Flint grinned.

He slowly eased the tip of his dick inside Dylan.

The lube made it more comfortable, and before long Flint was all the way inside. The perfect fit.

Dylan pushed his face down into the bed and began to groan. Flint knew how to work Dylan's body. His long, thick dick was made for this.

As he worked up the speed, Flint reached underneath Dylan and began to jerk his dick.

Maybe now was the time to give Dylan his orgasm.

And if Flint got the timing just right, maybe they could come together.

The pair of them were working in perfect unison.

Flint driving his manhood in and out of Dylan.

Dylan pushing back, making sure that every inch of Flint was inside him.

As Flint increased the pace, he also began to jerk Dylan's dick faster too.

'It's... happening!' Dylan squealed, his dick exploding with excitement all over the bedsheets at just the same time as Flint came inside him. 'Did you just... too?'

'I certainly did,' Flint said, using his final thrusts to drain himself completely. 'Wow. That was good. No, it wasn't good. It was *incredible*. Was it for you too?'

Dylan was lying on his back.

He looked overwhelmed. In a good way.

'*Uh-huh*,' Dylan said, barely able to speak. 'Nothing has ever come *close* to that. I guess I understand now why you do the whole orgasm thing?'

The pair of them laughed and embraced.

Climaxing at the same time was a great feeling and spoke volumes for their bond together. Both had come an awful long way and gone through so much in a short space of time.

They each had more learning and growing to do. That was normal. But the key thing was that they were going to be doing it together.

As a couple.

A perfectly matched, secure, and life-loving couple.

But as far as Flint was concerned, each and every step had been worth it. And then some more on top of that too.

Flint's journey had taken him from being a grouchy and cynical cop who couldn't enjoy life to something so much more rewarding.

He was a Daddy who lived to look after and please his Little.

Flint still might not have been totally satisfied with his role as a police detective. But as he closed his eyes and fell asleep, he had an idea.

It was potentially life changing for both him and Dylan too.

The type of idea that could mean a degree of upheaval but would be worth it if he could make it work.

But that could wait until morning.

Now it was all about snuggling up with Dylan and living for the moment.

Chapter Twenty-Three

Dylan knew he had slept soundly when he woke up the next morning feeling as fresh as a flower.

After a quick yawn and a stretch, Dylan looked across and saw that Flint was still fast asleep. And snoring loudly too...

Maybe it's a Daddy thing?

It's definitely kinda' cute though.

Even if it does mean I get woken up sometimes!

Dylan didn't want to wake Flint up. He knew that Flint was over-worked as it was. The more rest he could get, the better.

Without making so much as a single sound, Dylan eased himself off the bed and felt his feet touch the soft, fluffy rug under his feet.

The days of Flint's apartment being an ultra-sleek, minimalist bachelor pad were long gone. It was far more comfortable now. Rugs, paintings, and so much more color all over the place.

Dylan was happy that his influence was rubbing off on the apartment.

It truly was feeling like home.

A perfect space for a Daddy and Little to cohabit.

Dylan walked through the bedroom and towards the kitchen. He had a busy morning coming up so it was a case of very quietly making himself a bowl of multi-colored fruit loop cereal and munching that down as efficiently as he could.

Dylan prepared his stuffie Pinky a mini bowl of cereal too. This was part of his routine.

The only way he would start the day.

How could Dylan even *contemplate* eating himself if his best stuffie wasn't also getting his morning food?

Flint would tease him very gently about this. In Flint's estimation, the only reason Dylan prepared the extra bowl for Pinky was so that Dylan could get a few extra fruit loops for himself.

Flint may have had a point.

But there was no way that Dylan was going to admit that. Not even to his Daddy. He'd even risk a paddling to keep that secret intact.

But it wasn't just cereal that Dylan needed to take on board.

He made sure to eat a banana for a potassium boost.

Then take his multi-vitamins.

Oh, and then of course he remembered to prepare a cup of warm water and lemon to ensure that his voice was as well-prepared as possible for a busy morning of recording.

Dylan had been doing lots of research on how best to maintain his voice and have it as flexible and robust as possible for all of the voice work it would be doing.

This was Dylan's career now.

It was his passion too.

Dylan felt like he owed a great deal of thanks to Flint

who had been the one to encourage him and give Dylan the confidence to work hard and reach for his dreams.

Maybe the voice work would lead to other kinds of acting too.

Broadway was still part of Dylan's plans at some stage.

But right now, Dylan was getting a real sense of satisfaction from working as a voice actor.

He was honing his skills every day.

Attending workshops.

Putting together new showreels to demonstrate his range.

It was all so exciting.

Dylan just wished that Flint felt the same way about his work. Dylan knew that Flint had been a brilliant officer, and then detective. The police had given a lot to Flint in terms of building his skill sets and turning him into a confident and intelligent Daddy.

But Dylan could also see that the police work had worn Flint down. The death of Flint's partner had played a big role in that. But it was the never-ending workload and sometimes repetitive nature of things that Flint struggled with.

Dylan sighed.

Maybe one day Flint could find the same satisfaction as Dylan had in his work.

Speaking of which, Dylan finished off his cereal and walked into the small closet room that had been converted into his very own home studio.

Flint had arranged for it to be professionally soundproofed with the best quality materials. Dylan's computer and recording setup was absolutely perfect too.

It had actually been a lot of fun for Dylan to work on the technical side. It was a skill he never realized he had until he started committing to learning about it.

Again, this was another huge influence that had come from Flint. Dylan was now able to record and manipulate his voice to a high level. This included adding background sounds too. It could be a bustling New York street, or the calming sound of a mountain stream.

Pretty much anything was possible.

The escapism that it provided was great. Dylan loved being able to transport himself into the world of whatever story he was recording. Really immerse himself in whatever situation or scenario the story required.

This also applied to his steamier tales too.

There was still a huge thrill when it came to recording the naughtier parts of stories. A thrill that Flint loved to witness too. Indeed, the pair of them had found that after a recording session was one of their horniest times.

But there was no prospect of anything like that in this moment.

Dylan had far too much work to get through.

Dylan placed Pinky on his customized little Stuffie stool and began some vocal warm-up exercises.

Once he was done, he opened up the script file on his computer and began to record. It was a fun romance novel. One with just the right amount of angst and steam in it.

'This is going to be brilliant, Pinky!' Dylan exclaimed in between takes. 'Although sadly there isn't a part for a little pink stuffie!'

Dylan continued to record until he was suddenly disturbed by a sound behind him.

It was the studio door opening.

Dylan turned around and saw an apologetic looking Flint standing there.

'Sorry, buddy,' Flint said, still in his pajamas. 'Didn't mean to disturb you. We really should get a red warning light for outside the room. You know, like they have in professional studios?'

Dylan nodded.

It was another great idea from Flint.

'That sounds perfect, Daddy!' Dylan smiled. 'It's okay, you didn't disturb me really. I was about to take a break anyway. Shouldn't you be getting ready for work though?'

Flint smiled.

It was a broad, satisfied smile.

The kind of smile that radiated happiness.

'Hey, what's going on?' Dylan enquired, his mind working hard to try and figure out what was going on with Flint.

'Okay, I've been unhappy with work for a while. You know that?' Flint said, stepping into the studio and taking a seat next to Dylan.

'Yeah, I know Daddy.'

'Well, I was talking with Jackson and Luther and they inspired me,' Flint said, the excitement in his voice increasing. 'I'm going to hand in my resignation at the police department. I'll no longer be working for the city, but instead I'm going to open up my own private investigation practice. What do you think?'

Dylan took a minute to consider things.

But instinctively he knew it was a winning idea.

It all made sense.

Flint could continue investigating crime and helping people. But he wouldn't be tied into a system of working that didn't suit him any longer. He would also be free of the memories of his fallen partner.

'It sounds incredible!' Dylan beamed.

'I want to help people who the police can't,' Flint continued. ''You know, people like you. Littles. Anyone who doesn't feel like society is seeing things from their point of view. I'll judge no one. Only help them. Plus, I'll be able to work the hours that I decide. And go at the pace that suits me. It all makes so much sense.'

Dylan couldn't disagree with a single thing that Flint was saying.

It all sounded perfectly well thought and planned.

Exciting too.

Soon, both would be working for themselves and doing what they loved most.

It sounded corny, but Flint and Dylan would be living their personal dreams. And doing it together.

They'd have each other as a support network. Plus of course their friends at the Little Club and beyond.

'What's even better is that I can call on Jackson and Luther when I need specialist advice,' Flint said. 'A detective, doctor and firefighter working together? Maybe it's not so crazy to call ourselves the Hero Daddies after all.'

'I'm sure Casper will be very interested to know that you'll be spending more time with Jackson!' Dylan said, his mind returning to the thought that Casper and Jackson could be good for each other.

'Ha! Yes, but no interfering!' Flint warned. 'Too much matchmaking and I'll break out that paddle on your butt, Mister.'

They laughed heartily.

Dylan moved over and embraced Flint, squeezing as hard as he could.

It felt incredible to see Flint so happy with his work prospects. And having fun too and being lighthearted. Dylan knew that their kinks and sexual chemistry would always mean lots of paddlings and naughty fun, but seeing Flint so happy and relaxed about life was extra special.

'Okay, I'll see you later my perfect Little,' Flint said, standing up and heading towards the door. 'I need to get changed quickly. I've got an appointment down at the station with Sergeant Mase. I don't know how he's going to react to my news. Wish me luck!'

'Luck!' Dylan said, blowing Flint a kiss. 'You won't need it though. You've got it covered. You're my Daddy, you always know what to do.'

Flint smiled and left.

Dylan was now ready to get down to recording.

It was his first official take for this new project.

Dylan put on the headphones, hit record and began to speak...

'Once upon a time, there was a Little who needed a Daddy. And not just any Daddy. The best Daddy of all time.'

THE HERO DADDIES

Read all seven Hero Daddies books, including the brand new
seasonal novella Holiday Hero Daddy....

SAVING DYLAN

GUARDING CASPER

CLAIMING MILO

TAMING TIMOTHEE

OWNING AIDAN

DEFENDING JUSTIN

NEW: HOLIDAY HERO DADDY

MORE ZACK

Thank you *so much* for reading, I hope you had a great time!

If you'd love a **steamy & cute FREE story**, please sign up to my newsletter either by clicking **HERE** or copying and pasting the link below into your browser:

https://bit.ly/3KME5ra

I promise to never send spam emails. Only notifications of my upcoming releases and maybe even some super-fun little extras too!

Check out my **LITTLE CLUB NYC** series:

A LITTLE HEALING

A LITTLE FUN

A LITTLE SUBMISSION

A LITTLE RISK

Read my brand new **Gruff Guardian Daddies** novel:
DADDY RESCUE AT LITTLE RAPIDS

And introducing the **MAFIA DADDIES NYC** books:
TRAIN ME DADDY

CONTROL ME DADDY

AVENGE ME DADDY

I'm a new author, so **ratings and reviews on Amazon** massively help my books get seen! All ratings and reviews are hugely appreciated by me – thank you!

Following me on **Facebook** & **BookBub** yet? If not, come and join me! Get involved for news, updates and DDlb fun!

I love to hear from readers too, so please feel free to email me at zackwishauthor@gmail.com

Thank you and have a great day wherever you are!

Zack XoXo

Printed in Great Britain
by Amazon

25115076R00116

Saving Dylan

Hero Daddies
Book 1

Zack Wish

KEEP IN TOUCH

Thank you so much for reading, I hope you enjoy my book!

If you'd love a **steamy & cute FREE STORY**, and lots of *fun updates*, *freebies* and *more*, sign up to my newsletter by clicking the link below:

bit.ly/3KME5ra

I love to hear from readers too, so please feel free to email me at zackwishauthor@gmail.com

Stalk me at the places below too and make sure you don't miss a thing!